D1524123

ANYTHING
YOU
CAN DO

USA TODAY BESTSELLING AUTHOR
R.S. GREY

Copyright © 2017 R.S. Grey

All rights reserved. No part of this book may be reproduced or transmitted in any form, including electronic or mechanical, without written permission from the publisher, except in the case of brief quotations embodied in critical articles or reviews.

This book is a piece of fiction. Names, characters, places, and incidents are the product of the author's imagination or are used fictitiously. Any resemblance to actual events, locales, or persons, living or dead, is coincidental.

This book is licensed for your personal enjoyment only. This book may not be re-sold or given away to other people. If you are reading this book and did not purchase it, or it was not purchased for your use only, then you should return it to the seller and purchase your own copy. Thank you for respecting the author's work.

Published: R.S. Grey 2017
authorrsgrey@gmail.com
Editing: Editing by C. Marie
Proofreading: Jennifer at JaVa Editing
Cover Design: R.S. Grey
All rights reserved.
ISBN: 1542402085
ISBN-13: 9781542402088

R.S. Grey

For Lance

R⃥

CHAPTER ONE

I can't believe I'm here, back after so many years away. In all that time, I liked to imagine what this day would feel like, the day I returned victoriously to Hamilton, Texas, with a metaphorical gold medal around my neck. I always dreamed there would be a parade. Confetti, sparklers, cheap candy clipping the soft heads of children. At the very least, I assumed there would be a podium for me to stand on. I'm hopeful. Maybe in the time it has taken me to get ready, my mom has dragged one out of the hall closet.

I hear them all downstairs waiting for me. I am the guest of honor, the subject of the *WELCOME HOME, DR. BELL* sign taped over the fireplace. The party started an hour ago, and my mom has come up to check on me twice since then. Concerned. The first time I was spread out on my bed, prone, in a bathrobe I hadn't worn since high school.

"Better cinch that belt before you come down, Daisy. Your privates are trying to go public."

The second time, I was dressed, standing at my window and staring triumphantly at the two-story house next door. His house.

"If you're looking for Madeleine, she's already

1

downstairs."

"Her brother isn't here, is he?"

I know he's not. He's in California. Still, I need to hear her say it.

"No. Of course not."

I turn and narrow my eyes at her until I am sure she is telling the truth. That's what he does to me—makes me lose trust in my own mother. It's a side effect of being back in Hamilton, our old battlefield. Every square inch of this town is covered in our blood (red rover), sweat (cross country), and tears (see list). One time, just beneath the oak tree next door, I gave him a black eye when he told me no one was going to ask me to eighth grade formal. In the end, I went to the dance on the arm of *the* Matt Del Rey while he stayed home with a mushy bag of peas on his face.

I hadn't gotten off completely scot-free. After my mom heard about the punch, she marched me over to his front door to apologize. Unsatisfied by my sarcastic *soooorry*, our moms agreed that we needed to "hug it out". I remember pulling him into a sweet embrace and positioning my cheek softly against his so I could whisper a parting threat just out of parental earshot.

"If you ever tattle on me again, I'll make it two black eyes," I hissed.

He used his deceptive pubescent strength to squeeze my ribs like a boa constrictor, which our moms interpreted as geniality.

"I hope you get hit by the school bus," he whispered back.

"Daisy?" my mom says from the doorway, pulling my mind back to the present. "Are you ready to come down? Everyone is so anxious to see you."

I turn away from the window and stretch out my fist.

That incident took place fifteen years ago and my knuckle still aches sometimes. I wonder if his eye does too.

Downstairs, my mother has rounded up quite the motley crew of guests to welcome me back home: geriatric neighbors, out-of-touch friends, the little boy who delivers her newspaper. I know maybe half of the guests, but then again, I haven't called Hamilton "home" since before I left for college 11 years ago.

Everyone whoops and hollers when I make my appearance, my mom guiding them like an overzealous conductor from her spot at the base of the stairs.

"Welcome home, Doc!"

"Way to go, Daisy!"

There are claps on my back and drinks plopped in my hands. I don't usually love parties but tonight, I have something to celebrate. I'm finally realizing my dream: to take over my own private practice. It's the reason I'm back in Hamilton, the reason I put in so many years of hard work during medical school and residency.

I make my way to the kitchen to avoid doing shots with my middle school PE teacher, and there I find Madeleine on punch duty. As my oldest friend, I'm not surprised my mom has put her to work.

"I was wondering when you were going to come down. Wait, is that dress from high school?"

I shrug. "I haven't unpacked my suitcases yet, and I saw this hanging in the closet. It felt like a challenge."

She grins and flips some of her brown hair over her shoulder. "Well it looks way better on you now than it did back then."

On a bell curve of the female body type, I am somewhere left of center—thin, medium height, bony wrists. I developed boobs after high school, after everyone already had them and the novelty had worn off. Still, when I slipped into my dress upstairs and stood in front of my old full-length mirror, I was pleased to see I'd become my own teenage dream. Thank you, Katy Perry.

"You should have come upstairs."

She points to the half-empty punch bowl. "Your mom grabbed me as soon as I walked in."

"Leave the punch and let's take a bottle of wine out back. I bet we could down the whole thing before anyone finds us."

"You know we're adults now, right? We don't have to sneak alcohol anymore."

I shrug and reach around her for an unopened cabernet. "Yeah, but it's more fun to pretend that we do. Plus, I spotted Dr. McCormick on my way down and you know if he corners me, we're done for. He'll want to talk shop all night."

Madeleine's brown eyes go wide as saucers. "Oh god, you're right. Go. I'll grab glasses."

"Daaaaiiisssyyyyyy!"

My mom's singsong voice stops me dead in my tracks. My instincts tell me to drop the bottle and feign innocence, but then I remember I'm 28. Legal. Board-certified.

"Look what just arrived!"

I turn and nearly drop the bottle of cab. She is walking through the doorway of the kitchen holding a bomb.

"What. Are. Those?" I croak.

"They're flowers for you!" She beams. "Looks like a couple dozen."

Nearly three dozen to be exact. Fat, happy daisies. White.

"Get them out!"

"What? Don't be ridiculous! They were just delivered."

She is already bent over the kitchen sink, filling the massive vase with water. I wrench them out of her hand and water spills down the front of my thin dress. Now I'm everyone's teenage dream.

"Daisy!"

"No. No. No."

It is three steps to the backdoor, four to get down the stairs, and then I pitch the flowers into the trashcan out back. There, inside the bin, a small envelope taunts me from atop the discarded stems.

He is never one to overlook details; the envelope is a shade of pale pink that enrages me.

"Are you going to read it?" Madeleine asks. She's leaning over my shoulder, staring down at the envelope.

"No."

"Maybe it says something nice?"

I ignore her. As his sister, she can't help but want to defend him. She always has.

"How did he write it?" I ask.

"What?"

I keep my tone even. "If he is in California, how did he write the note? That," I point down, "is his handwriting."

"Oh. *Well...*"

"Madeleine."

"I thought you knew…"

My mouth is the Sahara. My words rasp out like a dry wind.

"You thought I knew what?"

"He's back. He moved back last week. I really thought

5

you knew."

Just like that, my parade is over, and confetti is stuck to my shoes.

I don't hate flowers; I hate *daisies*. They give me hives. They're the flower everyone wants me to be. The world sees me with my pale blonde hair and my big, shining blue eyes and they want to pat my head and plant me in their gardens. I'm not a daisy. I'm a doctor. I never want to be reduced to a daisy, and Lucas knows this better than anyone.

I drag Madeleine up to my room after I stuff the lid back on the trashcan. If Lucas has moved back to Hamilton, I need to know why. Like a chipmunk collecting nuts, I need to gather intel in my cheeks until they pop.

"Madeleine. Why is he back?"

"Well he's finished with residency, like you, so he came back for a job."

She isn't meeting my eyes.

"What job?"

She wrings out her hands, nervous.

"At Dr. McCorm—"

"NO!" I erupt. "*GOD NO!*"

She finally turns to me, her face twisted in sympathy. "I'm sorry, Daisy! I thought you knew! Why wouldn't Dr. M tell y'all you'd be working together?"

I hold my hand to my throat and feel my pulse—racing. I drop it and start to pace. There has to be an explanation. The facts are simple: Dr. McCormick owns the only family practice in town and he's hinted about retiring. His office is a one-man operation and he offered me a job during my last year of residency. Obviously, I took it, hence the celebratory parade.

So how the hell does Lucas factor into the equation? I clutch to a rapidly shrinking shred of optimism. Maybe Dr. McCormick needs an office manager, or better yet, a janitor.

Madeleine crosses in front of my path, momentarily stalling my paces. "Don't you think it's time you two put this weird animosity behind you? It's been 11 years. You're both on the cusp of becoming successful doctors. Surely you don't still hate each other!"

I laugh. It sounds hysterical.

"Madeleine, Madeleine, Madeleine."

"Stop saying my name."

"Do you remember when Mrs. Beckwith, the school counselor, pulled Lucas and me into her office during our senior year? After the parking lot incident?"

"No—"

"It took one hour for us to break her. She gave up counseling. Quit that same day, moved to upstate New York and started farming root vegetables. She said Lucas and I had—and I quote from her resignation letter—'robbed her of all faith in the future of humanity'."

"That sounds made up."

"I know your brother—probably much better than you do. We will never get along. 11 years apart is nothing. It has changed nothing. If anything, it's given our animosity time to mature like a fine wine—or better yet, a stinky cheese."

"Weren't you supposed to be studying medicine all this time?"

"Oh, believe me, I was. For every horrific skin disease,

cyst, and pustule we learned about, I imagined them on Lucas. For every slow, painful terminal illness, I pictured him suffering through them instead of just some nameless study participant. I was actually able to commit quite a lot to memory that way."

"You're hopeless." She throws up her hands and heads for the door. "I'm going down to hang out with your guests. You need to do some serious soul-searching, Daisy. Whether you like it or not, Lucas will be working with you at Dr. McCormick's, and I suggest you go in with a good attitude. Look at what he did today." She points to the pink envelope sitting on my bed. She'd dug it out of the trash before I could slam the lid down on her arm. I now regret not drawing blood. "Those flowers are clearly a peace offering—"

What a naïve girl, unhardened by a lifetime of continuous hostility.

"Oh please. They're a warning shot."

She rolls her eyes and walks out, leaving me alone in my Situation Room. The flowers are a secret message, his little reminder that nothing has changed between us. To everyone else, they look like a kind gesture. They can't see the subtext, the torture, and that is precisely his point.

I look down at the pink envelope then back at the open door. I am tempted to read it, so I close the door. I can hear my mom shouting at everyone to use coasters. No one will know.

Without hesitation, I tear into the envelope. His sharp script gives me tunnel vision.

Roses are red,
Daisy is you,
I heard you came back,
and I did too.

R̶x̶

CHAPTER TWO

Lucas Thatcher and I have been in competition with each other since day one. Yes, the actual day one, the day on which we were born, all of 58 minutes apart.

I crawled first. He spoke first. I walked first and he potty-trained first.

And so it went.

Our parents dressed us up in matching outfits and planned joint birthday parties. I've seen the photo albums, filled with two little infants: one a quiet angel, the other, a brash hellion. My favorite photo, one I liked to use as evidence, depicted us sitting side by side at a Halloween festival when we were almost a year old. They'd plopped us down on haystacks hoping for a sweet photo, but Lucas had turned on me, tearing off my small yellow bow with his uncoordinated infant fingers and throwing it on the ground. They'd snapped the photo just as I'd retaliated with the few teeth I wielded at the time.

Obviously infants aren't born with innate hatred pumping out of their tiny hearts, but I use our births as a starting point because nobody can pinpoint an exact date when our competition began. My mom swears we turned on one another when Lucas was chosen to be the preschool line leader. I tend to disagree—after all, you can't place all the blame on Mrs. Hallow, even if choosing Lucas over me was the biggest mistake of her entire career.

In light of the sheer longevity of our rivalry, people always want to know what terrible event had transpired to precipitate it all. The truth is, we've always been this way. I am the Annie Oakley to his Frank Butler and I firmly believe that anything he can do, I can do better.

A rivalry like ours sustains itself by constantly evolving. In elementary and middle school, the tactics were juvenile: vandalized finger paintings in art class, stolen soccer balls on the playground, sabotaged shoelaces in the school play.

These crude encounters inevitably produced a certain amount of collateral damage. Letters were sent home about school property and behavioral correction. I endured my first and only detention because of Lucas. We even lost friends—the ones who weren't willing to become lieutenants in our little war—but most importantly, we started to forfeit the respect of our teachers. As we grew older, we recognized the significance of these authority figures and the grades they doled out. The report cards sent home on thick white cardstock suddenly became our objective means of comparison, our apples to apples. Every six weeks those marks told us who was better, who was winning.

Now there are no more teachers, but there is Dr. McCormick, and I catch a lucky break when I run into him at Hamilton Brew the morning after the party.

I was planning on dropping by his house later, but this is better, *casual*. He sits in the corner near a window with the Sunday paper and a large coffee. I make note of the two empty sugar packets beside his cup.

He had seemed old to me in high school, but I now realize he's only got a year or two over my mother. His brown hair is salty and he's taken to growing out a white mustache. In all, I'd say he's a suave version of ol' Saint Nick.

"Dr. McCormick," I say with a winning smile. "Fancy seeing you here."

"Daisy!"

He's genuinely happy to see me, which I'm glad for. We shoot the breeze for a few minutes as only people from small towns can. There's rambling talk of a new housing development and a Wal-Mart.

"Next thing you'll know, we'll have a Whole Foods," he says with a shake of his head.

Without asking for permission, I sit down across from him and get down to business.

"I heard Lucas is back in town. Weird, right? I mean, what are the odds?"

My gaze is on the latte, but my attention is on him. He shifts awkwardly in his chair and reaches for his coffee. It's still steaming—too hot to drink—which means he's stalling.

"I thought I'd have another day of peace before you two found out."

My heart drops.

"So it's true? He's working with us?"

"Starting tomorrow, just like you."

I inwardly crumble, remember he's watching me, and force a smile.

"Can I ask why? Surely only one of us can take over the practice when you retire, right?"

He rubs his chin thoughtfully and I can't help but feel like I've overstepped my bounds. Still, he doesn't sidestep my question.

"To be honest, it wasn't something I planned, it just happened. I let it slip to a few people at church one Sunday that I was considering retirement, and wouldn't you know it, I had two emails and two voicemails waiting for me Monday morning."

"Me and Lucas?"

"Bingo. I guess that's what I get for opening my mouth."

I want to ask him who emailed him first, but I bite my tongue as he continues.

"I was proud that you two had both gone into family medicine, but shocked that you both wanted to return to little ol' Hamilton after all these years."

Lucas and I both had high enough scores for the more difficult specialties. Plastic surgery, dermatology—the few with flexible hours and big bucks. Family medicine spots aren't typically in high demand, or anyone's first choice.

"But as an old doctor is likely to do, I turned this problem on its head and looked at the silver lining. As you can see, Hamilton isn't as little as it used to be. Do you know I've had to skip lunch every day for the past five years just to meet the demand?"

I can see where he's going with this, and I don't like it. My fake smile is making my cheek muscles cramp.

"My point is, there's enough work for two doctors, maybe even three."

I don't need lunch. I'll work Saturdays—Sundays even. I want my own practice. It's my dream and he's slowly crushing it.

All I actually manage to say is, "Right."

I try not to let dread show on my face. I moved back to Hamilton a few days ago assuming the practice was as

14

good as mine, but part of being a doctor is being able to roll with the punches and adapt when things don't go according to plan. So, I conjure up a genuine smile and resolve to fix this later.

I scoot my chair back, stand, and stretch my hand out across the table.

"Well Dr. McCormick, whatever ends up happening, I look forward to practicing with you."

He grins, pleased.

As I leave Hamilton Brew, I take an espresso shot to-go...then think ahead and grab another. Tomorrow morning, I will come face to face with my rival, and there are a few things I need to take care of before then.

From Hamilton Brew, I walk down Main Street and head into the biggest salon in town. I haven't trimmed my hair in almost a year. That won't do. I ask for clean layers and have them shape it so it frames my delicate features. From there, I ask for every spa treatment they have. I don't want to be pretty for Lucas, who, as a robot, isn't programmed to register beauty. The primping is all for me. I'm a general preparing for battle, and while they buff my feet, I flip through my old medical textbooks, brushing up on the off chance I encounter some obscure, hard-to-pronounce illness tomorrow.

"What about your brows? Want us to shape them up a bit?"

I laugh because it's a stupid question. "Yes. Do it. All of it."

When I stroll into my mom's house later, she's sitting at the dining table flipping through magazines and talking on the phone. She looks up at me as I close the door and her mouth falls open in shock.

"I'll have to call you back," she says into the phone.

"Someone that looks like Daisy just got home."

I drop my shopping bags on the couch and walk into the kitchen. I'm taking a massive bite out of an apple when she comes in to join me. She's petite, even more so than I am. Her blonde hair hides the few grays she has, and her regimented skincare routine means she looks 30 instead of 50. Usually her smile can light up a room, but right now, it lights up nothing.

"You've been busy today," she says, waving her hand up and down my body. I'm not really the girly-girl type; there was no time for it during medical school and residency. This woman with glossy hair and smooth legs seems foreign even to me, but it feels good, as if I'm faster and more aerodynamic now that they've stripped most of the hair from my body.

"What's in the shopping bags?" she asks as I munch on my apple.

"Work clothes."

She arches a brow. "I thought you told me the other day you didn't need anything."

"That was before—" I hold my tongue and then pivot. "I just changed my mind. These clothes are new and I spent all afternoon with Mrs. Williams getting them altered."

She smirks. "So you *do* know, don't you?"

"About what, *Mother*?"

The use of the word mother hints at my annoyance with her, like when she uses my full name.

She rubs her temple and sighs. "I only found out a few days before you moved back. I was going to tell you, but I'm a selfish woman and I wanted you back here. You've been gone too long."

"You still should have told me."

She nods, agreeing. "I take it from the clothes that

16

you're not leaving?"

"Do you think I should?"

"Absolutely not."

"Do you want to see what I bought then?"

It's an olive branch and she takes it readily. Truthfully, I'm not that upset that she didn't tell me Lucas moved back sooner; I understand her reasoning. She and I have always been close, especially since it was just the two of us for so many years after my dad got sick when I was little. She hardly wanted me to leave for college and now that I'm back, I have no plans to leave this town again. No, McCormick Family Practice is as good as mine.

We're upstairs in my room picking out my outfit for my first day of work when my phone rings on the nightstand. It's a number I don't recognize and I nearly ignore it, but curiosity gets the better of me.

Waving my mom out, I lock the door and answer.

"Hello?"

"Daisy Bell."

I haven't heard his voice in 11 years.

"May I ask who's calling?"

"I think you know."

"Lucas Thatcher. I don't recognize the number. Am I your one call from jail?"

"I called from a payphone. I don't want you tracing this."

"It's 2017—where did you find a payphone?"

"That's irrelevant. Listen, we haven't seen each other in a long time, and I wanted to break the ice. I don't want things to get ugly tomorrow."

"I don't have any clue what you're talking about. I'm looking forward to working together, Lucas."

"Y'know, after all these years, I can still tell when

you're lying—but it doesn't matter. This is your chance to bow out, Daisy. Gracefully. You can tell everyone you got another job."

"You'll be the one bowing, Lucas, when Dr. McCormick sees the mistake he's made in hiring you."

"Not likely."

"I'm going to bring him snickerdoodles. Dr. McCormick *loves* snickerdoodles."

"We're going golfing on Saturday and I'm going to let him win."

"You hate losing."

"Only to you."

"Well then the next few months won't be very pleasant for you."

"Are you done? I'm about to have to put in another quarter."

"I'm surprised you didn't call collect and make me pay."

I think I hear him chuckle, but it could be a crackle from the ancient payphone.

"I'll see you in the morning then, Dr. Bell."

I open my mouth, but then decide to end the call without dignifying him with a response.

Not if I see you first.

℞

CHAPTER THREE

It was a shock to no one that Lucas and I both took the pre-med track in college. What career path is worth pursuing more than medicine? Perhaps law, but neither of us had enjoyed the mock trials we suffered through in Ms. Pace's ninth grade history class. The only reason we'd put any effort into it at all was because we were pitted against one another, opposing counsel. I'd won, offering up a closing argument so good Atticus Finch would have been proud. Ms. Pace had consumed a heroic amount of Excedrin that year.

Our senior year of high school, Lucas was offered a full ride to Stanford. Duke extended me the same. The fact that our universities were on opposite coasts further cemented our choices. In fact, I'd have gone all the way to New Zealand if they had offered me a full ride.

After I moved away for college, information about Lucas was only offered up by Madeleine. We had an unspoken rule wherein I never asked about him and she brought him up often, as if I cared what he was doing with his life. She was the one to tell me when he was visiting home so I could stagger my visits. Once I confirmed that Lucas was away, I'd return home in short, anxiety-ridden bursts. The idea of him popping up in our small town at any time made it impossible to enjoy the holidays.

Due to my careful planning and Madeleine's incredibly detailed calendar, I haven't seen Lucas in 11 years, not even in photos. I don't use Facebook. One night in college, I decided I didn't need the distraction any longer and disabled my account. Sure, earlier that same night Lucas had been tagged in a photo with a pretty blonde at a winter formal at Stanford, but that was unrelated to my decision. It really is a stupid website.

The fact that I'm going to come face to face with Lucas after so many years apart makes it impossible to sleep, so I don't bother. I get out of bed at the crack of dawn and get ready for work. My outfit—fitted gray cigarette pants, black blouse, and matching ballet flats—is professional, but also comfortable enough for a long day filled with appointments. Once my hair and makeup are done, I ride my bike the short distance to Hamilton Brew. The coffee shop is right across the street from the office and I have a perfect vantage point to watch for when Lucas arrives. I think it's important that I see him before he sees me; I want every advantage I can get.

The barista brings me two coffees (one for me and one for Dr. McCormick) and makes a joke about my morning read: *The American Journal of Medicine*. It's no *Cosmo*, but the articles will distract me for a little while. My heart is racing and I haven't even had caffeine yet. I blame it on my bike ride.

"Daisy Bell, is that you?"

I turn and stare up into the face of a girl I haven't seen since my high school graduation.

"Hannah?" I toss out hopefully. Without Facebook, I have to rely on my memory.

She beams and I know I'm right.

"How are you?" she asks, stepping closer with a big, confident smile.

I nod. "I'm good, yeah. How about you?"

I see her diamond-studded hand rubbing her very pregnant belly.

"I'm good. Eight months along and not really sleeping much at the moment."

That's why she's at the coffee shop at a time usually reserved for shift workers and crazy doctors staking out their nemeses.

"Congratulations, you look great."

She rolls her eyes in disbelief.

"Well that's polite of you to say. Todd says I've never looked better, but I think he's just saying—"

"Todd Buchanan?!"

She nods with a laugh. "The same! We got married a few years back."

I feel like I've stepped into the twilight zone. My classmates are getting married and having children. I'm 28 and have never declared my love for a significant other. My biggest commitment so far is buying a Roomba. How is this possible? How am I so behind?

"That's great," I croak.

"God, you look different," she spouts, waving her hand from the top of my blonde hair to the tip of my ballet flats. "I mean, you used to be pretty in high school, but you never quite knew what to do with all that hair and those freckles. I'm glad you don't cover them up."

I touch my cheek, a little shocked by her candidness. "Thanks."

"Y'know, I saw Lucas the other day," she continues. "Moving his stuff upstairs."

My body hums. I tell myself it's the caffeine kicking in, though I haven't taken a sip. Must be the fumes.

"Oh?"

This is news to me; I assumed he would be moving back in with his parents temporarily. Lucas and I lived next door to one another our entire lives. Our proximity didn't matter much when we were younger, but as soon as we entered high school, that changed. There was no escape. We knew each other's every move. No boy ever picked me up for a date without Lucas lingering outside, somehow ruining the moment. Checking the mail, mowing the lawn, washing his car—innocuous activities that did little to hide his true intent: to get inside my head and ruin the moment.

I wasn't quite as bold. I used the perch at my bedroom window to spy when the moments presented themselves, like when he kissed Carrie Kocher on his front porch when we were fourteen. I'd been glued to the pane of glass, watching and trying to suppress my gag reflex. *How can she stand it?* I'd wondered.

I reach for my coffee, examine the milky brown color, drop it, shuffle it a little to the left, and then look back to Hannah. She is wearing a little smirk and then she leans down close so the barista can't hear.

"He's still the hottest thing to come out of Hamilton High."

If I'd taken a sip of my coffee, I would have performed a spit take all over her face.

"I take it from your reaction you two still don't get along?" she continues.

I'm not shocked she remembers our rivalry. I think the Bush administration was briefed about our antics at one point.

"Can someone that arrogant get along with anyone?" I

joke, trying to push the blame where it belongs: on Lucas.

She laughs. "You were the only one to have a problem with him. We never could figure it out. There was even a rumor going around that—"

I laugh loudly and aggressively. I need her to shut up and go have her baby somewhere.

"Well, I don't want to keep you, and I need to get back to reading…"

She takes the hint and steps back. I wish her luck with her pregnancy and then go back to pretending to read my journal. It's only when she walks out that I realize I never asked her what she meant by "moving his stuff upstairs."

I'd heard they were putting lofts in some of the second stories along Main Street, but…surely he isn't right above me right now. My spine trembles and I slowly raise my eyes to the ceiling, as if expecting drops of blood to drip on my forehead like in a horror movie.

Instead I see only exposed ductwork and wiring, and I feel like a fool. I've thought about Lucas for longer than I care to. It feels like I'm already losing a competition that doesn't even exist, so for the next few minutes, I pretend I'm back at Duke, a million miles away from Lucas. The daydream does wonders for my nerves, and I can almost imagine a world in which he doesn't exist.

After I've settled into the Oscar-worthy impression of calm I'm determined to exude, a door opens outside, adjacent to the coffee shop's front entrance. I scrunch my brows and lean closer to the window, watching in slow motion as a man walks out onto the sidewalk. A man I'd hoped to avoid for a lifetime, or at least another five minutes. A man who is the very bane of my existence.

R.S. Grey

℞
CHAPTER FOUR

My mouth dries. My hands shake. My stomach plummets and then flips over and over like a rollercoaster set to MAX SPEED. Technically, I'm getting my wish—I'm seeing him before he sees me—but my wish has changed and I want him to disappear, to go back up to his hidey-hole and stay there forever.

His back is to me and I begin an assessment of him that's purely scientific. His hair is dark brown, thick and trimmed by someone who knows what they're doing. He's wearing navy slacks and a crisp white button-down. His brown leather watch matches his belt and shoes. At some point over the years, a woman must have taught him how to color coordinate, presumably before he chopped her up and turned her into jerky.

He turns to look both ways before crossing the street. He doesn't do it because it's what his mother taught him—I know he's looking for me, ensuring I'm not waiting with a souped-up Ford Bronco, prepared to mow him down. For a few seconds, I'm provided with a view of his profile. Of course. I curse time and testosterone. 11 years have taken his chubby cheeks and sharpened them to hard lines. They've stretched his tall frame and blown it up like a muscled balloon. Without a doubt, he eats protein and has a gym membership.

In high school, he preferred contact lenses. Now, he is wearing thick black frames like he has an audition for some new superhero movie after work and he's trying to step into the role early. *Pathetic.* They suit him.

Once he's sure the coast is clear, he takes a step out onto the street. Soundlessly, I rise and tail him like an undercover cop. When I slip out of the coffee shop, Lucas doesn't turn, but he immediately spots me in the reflection of the plate glass that fronts McCormick Family Practice— my hair is too bright to go unnoticed. Our eyes lock in the mirrored surface and neither of us turns or wavers. We're the only ones out on the street; I could scald him with Dr. McCormick's coffee and claim it was an accident. It would be his word against mine, and I'm adorable, but this coffee already has a purpose.

Our steps clap in unison, left, right, left, right. I desperately yearn to touch the door handle first, a tiny achievement, but it's impossible unless I break into a sprint. Too desperate even for me. He reaches the door first and I predict he will step inside and lock it behind him. Instead, he steps back and holds it open for me.

I know it's just an act. Chivalry is dead. Lucas killed it.

When I'm a step away from brushing past him, he smiles coyly and sticks his foot out to trip me. Without breaking stride, I take an exaggerated step over it.

"Did you like the flowers?" he asks.

His voice is deeper and smoother than it was on the phone, like a dark liquor, the kind that leaves you with a nasty hangover.

I smile. "They're rotting in the garbage."

"And the card?" His malevolent tone confirms the

flowers and the card were less of a gift, and more of a Trojan horse into my psyche.

"It burned nicely."

Our first encounter in 11 years is sharp. I'm not surprised we're picking up right where we left off.

We step into the lobby and Dr. McCormick is waiting for us with the rest of the staff. They're wearing eager smiles and I don my own, careful to tilt my head away from Lucas so he can't see.

"WELCOME DOCTORS!" they all shout, pointing to the homemade banner hanging behind the reception desk.

My smile widens as our boss steps within earshot. "Good morning, everyone! Dr. McCormick, I brought your usual from The Brew. As for everyone else, the first coffee break is on me today."

They are pleasantly surprised and Lucas is not. I extend the coffee out to our boss and finally turn to glance up at Lucas. My smile seems genuine because up until a second ago it was. I've learned a few tricks over the years.

Lucas evaluates me. He drags his dark gaze from the tip of my ballet flats to the top of my shiny hair; he's wondering if I'm still a worthy opponent. When the edge of his mouth slowly unwinds into a smirk, I know he's excited to have his old rival back. He wants to pick the meat from my bones.

Dr. McCormick goes through introductions and while Lucas gives everyone a handshake and a smile, I do more. I commit their names to memory and begin to build a plan of attack for each and every one of them. There are two medical assistants, one nurse, and one office manager. Everyone but the office manager looks young, around my age, and they are all female, all enamored with Lucas right away. It's biology and I cannot compete, so I try another

27

tactic.

"Those are adorable scrubs, Casey."

The nurse beams with my approval.

Gina, the office manager, walks around the reception desk and takes two white coats off the rack. There's one for Lucas and one for me. Lucas grabs for both and mine looks ridiculously small in his hands as he holds it open for me.

"I didn't realize they came in child sizes," he says, holding it out to me with a devilish smirk.

I grit my teeth and hold my tongue while the women of the office giggle as if his joke is funny. I'll have my work cut out for me with this group. Grudgingly, I slip one arm in and turn my back to him. He steps forward as my other arm fills the sleeve, and it's the closest we've been in 11 years. He adjusts the back of my collar and his fingers brush the back of my neck.

His helpful attempt to unsettle me backfires. With my white coat on, I feel intimidating and in charge. It's embroidered with the logo for McCormick Family Practice on one side and Daisy Bell, M.D. on the other. Dr. McCormick stares between the two of us, tears brimming his eyes. He's a big softie.

"It goes without saying that I'm proud of the two of you."

I scoot a little closer to him and Lucas follows.

"Time for the rundown. I figure we'll do a probationary period where you two get the lay of the land. You both did residencies in big cities and you'll find that small town practices are different. Here, there are no specialists for 50 miles around. You'll see it all, and I need to know you both can handle that."

"And if one of us can't handle it, what happens?" I ask innocently. Maybe I still have a chance at owning my own practice. My dream isn't completely dead.

"Oh I doubt that will happen. You're both capable physicians. This break-in period is more for my benefit than for yours. It's going to be hard to let go."

He's skirting around it, but the fact is, he really thinks Lucas and I will be sharing the practice. I think someone spiked his breakfast with crazy pills.

"I've noticed you both seem to have...reservations about sharing the practice. I didn't mean it to be some kind of trick, so I won't hold either of you to your contract if you'd like to accept a job elsewhere. I know you both had plenty of offers."

He doesn't know me at all if he thinks I'll bow out now that Lucas Thatcher is my coworker. If anything, I'm more committed to this job than ever before.

"Of course not. Thank you for this opportunity," I say sincerely.

"I won't take this position lightly," Lucas follows. There are audible sighs.

Dr. McCormick chuckles and wipes at a tear that nearly falls down his cheek. Then, with a nod, he transitions the office back into work mode. "All right, well let's get going. It'll be a busy day. We've already notified the patients ahead of time that their provider will be changing. I'll see them if they insist on it, but sooner or later, they'll have to get used to you two being here."

No, they'll have to get used to me, and they will— happily. My bedside manner is excellent. I'm gentle and understanding. I'm a good listener, unlike Lucas. I'll bet he sighs heavily and looks at his watch during appointments. I'll bet he rushes his patients, hurrying them along when they try to give him their full history.

"If you'll follow me," Gina starts. "I'll show you two to

your offices."

I beat Lucas to the door off of the reception area. He retaliates by striking up a conversation with Gina. I hold back, hoping Gina sees through his transparent efforts to endear himself to her. From the sparkle in her eyes, I suspect she's happy to be a pawn as long as the king looks like *that*.

Our offices are small, basically two closets stacked side by side near the back of the building. They've refitted them for our use and I go on about how nice they are. I think Gina is a bit suspicious of my enthusiasm. I can hardly turn around in the small space and there's a stack of boxes all but blocking the doorway.

"Right. Well, the kitchen is there," she says, pointing behind her. "I make coffee in the mornings, but let me know if it's running low and I'll make more. Don't leave dishes in the sink and clean up after yourselves. I'm the office manager, not the maid."

"I'm a coffee fiend, but I'm happy to make my own," Lucas says with a perfected smile.

She nods before she turns away, seemingly appreciating his down-to-earth attitude. It's fake. Once she's turned the corner back down the hallway, he and I are left alone for the first time. We stand side by side in the doorways to our offices, not moving. Our arms are crossed, and though I try to stand with my shoulders as straight as possible, he's still got a foot on me.

"You haven't changed one bit," he finally says.

"Really? Because you've gotten much worse."

"You're probably right." He finally turns to face me and I'm stunned by just how handsome the years have made him. He has a defined jaw, straight nose, and alluring brown eyes. It doesn't seem fair. He tilts his head and I blink, aware that I've likely been staring for too long. "Listen Daisy, I know we have had our differences in the past, but we've both grown up and I just hope we can turn over a new leaf. Neither of us wants to jeopardize this opportunity, so let's just leave the childish antics behind."

His heartfelt speech sounds genuine, and for a moment, I wonder if it is—but then his wicked smirk betrays him. It's insidious. A lesser woman might have believed him, but I snap his olive branch over my knee.

"I'm touched, Lucas. Did you practice that in front of your mirror last night?"

Before he can continue with his mind tricks, I turn and shut my office door. The room is thimble-sized, nearly too small for me, which means the one next door is definitely too small for Lucas. The image of him crammed inside there spreads a smile across my lips.

I drop my bag and stare down at the patient list printed out for me. There are 24 patients on the docket for the day. Eight of them are seeing Dr. McCormick, and the other 16 are divided between Dr. Thatcher and Dr. Bell.

An idea springs to mind and my hands shake with a burst of adrenaline. I turn from my desk and rip open my door, nearly sprinting back to reception.

Dr. McCormick's probationary period is our chance to prove ourselves to him. I can continue to butter him up with coffee and compliments, and I will, but that is only Phase I of my plan: win the love of Dr. McCormick. If I ever want to realize my dream of owning the practice outright, I need to make Lucas seem like the odd man out amongst the two other groups in the equation: the office staff, and the patients. With the office staff consisting primarily of women, Lucas will inevitably have the upper hand. Apparently, most women seem to find his type attractive, and unless I am prepared to permanently disfigure his face, there is no changing that. Our patients, however, will be males and females of all ages. They will want a pleasant, compassionate doctor regardless of gender or muscle definition. If I can sway the patients to my side and Dr. McCormick hears them raving about me, he will have to rethink his decision to include Lucas in his legacy. The staff and patients are constituents in a democracy, and I will win their vote. Lucas will win a bus ticket out of town.

So begins Phase II: win the love of the office staff and patients.

I pass the two medical assistants, Mariah and Becky, as they prep the exam rooms for our patients. I smile extra wide. Gina and Casey are both sitting behind the front desk, working. Beside Gina's computer, there is a bin full of the files for the patients coming in today. There are eight files there that I need to read, eight patients who range from slightly annoyed to very angry at the fact that their physician is retiring. They're nervous and I will hold their hands and walk them through this period of change. By the time I'm done with them, they won't even remember who Dr. McCormick was.

I'm quietly going over my patient histories when Mariah and Becky return to reception with fresh coffee in their mugs. *Phase II*, I think to myself, clearing my throat.

"So I know I only brought Dr. McCormick coffee this morning, but I was hoping you'd all join me for a coffee break sometime this week, my treat." I sparkle. "Just us girl—"

The door chime aborts my kind gesture. I lean over the reception desk and narrow my eyes on a young kid carrying in two hefty bags. He has a hat on backward and eyes that say he'd rather be sleeping.

"Oh! Are those for us?" Gina stands and claps her hands with glee.

"They aren't for me." The kid shrugs and then looks down at the note in his hand. "They're a delivery from some guy named Lucas."

"It's Dr. Thatcher," Gina corrects him with a scowl.

The kid shrugs; at seven bucks an hour, he clearly could not care less. He wants his tip, which Lucas hands him from over my shoulder. I didn't notice his approach and now I find myself more than a little annoyed at him for thinking of such a brilliant idea. I smell donuts, and everyone likes donuts, especially me.

"Oh, and one more thing from a..." The kid checks his note again. "Daisy."

I glare back at Lucas, but his face is a mask of obliviousness. What game is he playing?

"That's so sweet, you two!" Casey says, going around the desk to take the two bags from the kid so he can scurry out of the office.

The entire office trails her back to the kitchen and we watch as she unloads the two bags. In one, there are four boxes of warm donuts, glazed and iced within the last few minutes. There is visible steam rising off them.

"Those are from me," Lucas says with a small smile.

In the other bag, Casey unwraps a sickly fruit display and I feel everyone's smiles fall.

"And that's from Daisy," Lucas chimes in. "Thoughtful, right?"

The vile, off-brand Edible Arrangement sports a collection of sad, droopy melons and the occasional mushy grape impaled on a wooden skewer. It is decomposing as we speak, the color of pale flesh.

"Oh, um, what a nice idea, Dr. Bell!" Casey says

through a mouthful of chocolate sprinkles. She plucks an oversized toothpick out of the display and barely covers her marked repulsion.

I stand in the doorway as each staff member slides past the buffet, loading their plates up with donuts and skipping right past the soggy fruit Lucas has attributed to me.

"Oh, I already had a fruit serving this morning," Gina explains, not meeting my eyes as she glides out of the kitchen.

"I'll…uh, come back for some of yours later, Daisy," Mariah promises weakly.

When it's Becky's turn, she audibly gags as she passes the fruit display, just barely stifling her throw-up. She doesn't even offer an excuse before taking two donuts.

Lucas and I are alone in the kitchen and I'm shaking with rage. I'm not even upset with him—I'm upset with myself. I've underestimated him and I won't let it happen again.

He steps around me, reaching for a small white paper bag I'd overlooked before. It's a special delivery and he holds it right out to me.

"Bavarian cream."

I want to smash it in his face and cloud his lenses.

"I've already had breakfast."

My stomach grumbles in dissent, but he doesn't mention it.

"Right. I'll just leave it right here." He holds eye contact as he drops the bag back on the counter. His eyes are light brown, the color of walnuts. It's no coincidence I've never been able to stomach that particular nut.

My morning passes with awkward patient encounters and secret, spiteful bites into the Bavarian cream donut I was forced to accept. I take the last bite just as Lucas walks by my office, and he surveys me suspiciously.

"Granola bar," I say as flecks of carbohydrates escape my lips.

"Nobody's accusing you," he says. "But if you're not going to eat that donut I gave you, I'm sure Dr. M would like a bite. Can I have it back?"

"Oh, I had to toss it—it smelled like the cream had soured," I mumble in between swallows.

Around lunchtime, Dr. McCormick calls us into his office. I assume it's because he's already made his decision and has decided to let Lucas go.

"Sit down, you little rock stars." He waves to the worn leather chairs in front of his desk.

Lucas graciously holds out his arm to indicate I should sit first. I watch carefully as I sit, just on the off chance that he's planning to yank the chair out from under me. I doubt he would stoop to such depths in front of Dr. McCormick, but after this morning's little stunt, I take nothing for granted.

"As much as I appreciated the little banquet this morning, I don't want you two to think you need to bring in treats every day to get on my good side." He pats his stomach as if to say his health won't hold up if our gamesmanship continues. "Although my truck *is* due for an oil change, if you really wanted to earn my favor," he adds with a laugh.

Lucas rolls up his white coat sleeves as if he's about to pop the hood of Dr. McCormick's car himself. "Conventional or synthetic?"

Kiss-ass.

"I'll tell you what I really want to see out of you two: warmth, and investment in your neighbors. You see, I pride myself on running a practice that engages with the community. Too often, doctors get so caught up in making money that they forget the reason they got into medicine in the first place, which is to help people. Tell me, do either of you remember the fourth line of the Hippocratic Oath?"

Lucas and I glare at each other nervously before shaking our heads.

"I wouldn't expect you to, but it holds a special meaning for me, so I've got it hangin' right here." He points to a framed print on the wall behind him. "'I will remember that there is art to medicine as well as science, and that warmth, sympathy, and understanding may outweigh the surgeon's knife or the chemist's drug'," he recites.

I nod reverently. "That's my favorite part."

Lucas stares into the side of my head and I can feel the waves of disdain rolling off him.

"You kids are fresh out of residency, and while I'm sure you think you know what it means to be a family doctor, be assured that you still have a lot to learn. In a small town like this, generations pass before your very eyes. From this humble office, I've watched children grow up and start bringing in children of their own. I've been with old folks when they die. I guess what I'm trying to say is that you'll become more than just a doctor to these people, you'll become a part of their families. Do you two think you can handle that kind of responsibility?"

I've leaned so far forward during his speech that I nearly fall off my chair when I nod.

"Yes," Lucas and I say in unison.

"Good. Then for the next few months, I'm going to challenge you. I want to see passion, even when I'm throwing my toughest patients at you. I want to see innovation, to see that you're not just going through the motions like so many doctors do these days. Surprise me! I want you to be the best!"

The energy radiating off Lucas and me is palpable. We are the Titans and Dr. McCormick is Denzel. I want to bang my helmet against the locker room wall and yell HOORAH.

"I won't let you down, sir," Lucas says, standing.

I clamor to my feet and step toward the desk with my hand outstretched. "My entire life has led up to this moment."

Dr. McCormick smiles at each of us and then we are excused for our afternoon appointments. There was tension before, but Dr. McCormick has just ratcheted it up to unprecedented levels. He has blown the starter pistol and we sprint out of his room, pushing each other down the long hallway.

"You're going to embarrass yourself if you stay," I taunt.

We're feet away from our individual offices and I'm thinking I'm going to escape inside when he turns and cages me in against the wall. I don't cower; I press right up against him, tilting my head back to stare into his ugly walnut eyes.

He reaches out and fingers the patch on my white coat. "When you're packing your bags in a few weeks, I'll let you keep this coat so you can always remember what might have been."

I think he can feel my heart racing beneath the fabric. Infuriating. I don't have a good enough comeback, so I go on the offensive.

"Did you hear him in there? He's not looking for a golfing buddy, he's looking for warmth." I brush down the side of his face with the velvet back of my hand. "And what could be warmer than a woman's touch?"

Aside from a twitch of his cheek, he is unmoved.

"Was that really your favorite part of the oath?"

"If it's Dr. McCormick's favorite, then it's mine too," I say with an innocent smile.

His eyes narrow. "I didn't realize you were a puppet now. If I stick my hand in you, will you do my bidding as well?"

Mariah coughs politely and we're suddenly aware of her presence at the end of the hall. "Sorry to interrupt sir, er…ma'am, Dr. Bell, but Mrs. Harris is ready to see you in room three."

I smile and duck under Lucas' arm like we're done, but we're far from it. I brush past Mariah, thank her for the chart, and walk away from the firefight before a stray shot clips me on the way out. As soon as I turn the corner, my confident smile drops.

It is time to initiate Phase III: force Lucas out.

At 6:00 PM, I straighten up my desk and begin to pack up. The few leftover donuts are quickly claimed, and Gina loads me up with the fruit display that may as well have cartoonish stink lines drifting up from it.

"Can you take this home? It's attracting flies."

I smile tightly and nod my head, moving to the front door with the fruit display in hand. I parked my bicycle outside of The Brew earlier and it's still there, its cheerful, mint green paint taunting me.

"Good work today, Dr. Thatcher!" Gina says from behind me.

"Great first day!" Casey chimes in.

They're patting him on the back as he leaves and if I turn around, I will barf.

I push through the front door of the office and he follows behind me. For a second I think he's up to no good, but then I remember he lives across the street. How convenient.

I pick up my pace, hurrying to put distance between us. The two-way street is small and my bike is so close; I can taste freedom.

I bound off the sidewalk and tires squeal. I hear an ear-splitting *HONK* and Lucas Thatcher is there, grabbing my elbow and tugging me back before I collide with the front bumper of the delivery truck careening down the street.

"Watch it!" the driver yells out the window.

I shake my head and blink rapidly.

My heart is jumping out of my chest. My breaths are short, quick gasps. I vaguely register that I'm shaking with shock.

"Don't make this too easy for me," Lucas teases.

His arm is still squeezing me and for one long second, I close my eyes and stand there, letting him hold me. The second passes quickly though and then my shock is replaced with white-hot rage, directed at myself. How stupid can I be, not even looking both ways before crossing the street?

I yank myself out of his hold. "It's probably not the first time someone has jumped into traffic after spending a day with you."

It's a nice recovery, but I still can't believe he just saved me. How disturbing.

After checking for traffic, I run across the street and stuff my bag and the fruit in my bike's wicker basket. Fuming, I strap my helmet on and pull my bike off the rack a little more aggressively than intended. The evening sun is beginning to dip low on the horizon, and as I pedal west toward home, I'm nearly blinded. Somehow, this is Lucas' fault too.

A half-mile in, my heart rate increases, and his words form an echo chamber in my head.

You haven't changed one bit, Daisy...

The fruit is from Daisy...

I didn't realize you were a puppet now...

I begin to take my frustration out on the bike, pounding against the pedals with as much force as my legs can muster, all while imagining them to be Lucas' sensitive parts.

Powered by my rage, I build up an impressive amount of speed as I come upon my final turn onto Magnolia Ave. I lean into the turn to compensate for my momentum, and my worn tires bite into the pavement.

Until they don't.

I hit an oil slick, a gift to the environment from one of Hamilton's many old, leaky farm trucks. My back tire fishtails, and my handlebars wobble in a futile effort to right the floundering ship. Time slows down as my bike, now perpendicular to my direction of travel, buckles sideways and loads me up like a circus performer in a cannon. Time speeds up just before my impact with the street.

My brain jumps into action, forcibly volunteering my left arm to take the full brunt of the fall. Valiantly, the limb springs out at the last second as if to tell the road to *talk to the hand*. Sadly, the road has a lot to say. I hear a sickening crack just above the overall clamor of the crash, and then an abrupt silence settles over the scene.

R.S. Grey

℞
CHAPTER FIVE

"Nice cast," Lucas says the next morning.

"Don't talk to me."

"Did they let you pick the color?"

It's neon green, my favorite.

"No," I lie. "It's all they had."

"Morning," Gina says with a smile, doing a poor job of surreptitiously ogling Lucas. He's wearing a light blue dress shirt that compliments his tan skin, and apparently Gina thinks it looks good on him. I hadn't noticed.

Lucas and I have been standing in the small kitchen for the last few minutes, waiting for the coffee to finish brewing. I swear it is percolating even slower than usual.

"Oh no! Dr. Bell, what happened?"

She has finally pulled her gaze off Lucas long enough to notice the lime green elephant in the room.

"Bike accident yesterday." I shrug, holding up my fractured wrist. "The ground came out of nowhere."

Other than that, I've got a few tender ribs and a nice gash across my forehead, which is currently covered by a matching neon green Band-Aid. As soon as I leave the kitchen, I'll exchange it for a boring beige to throw Lucas off my scent.

Dr. McCormick steps up behind Gina and shakes his head. "Sorry to hear about the accident, Daisy. Your mom called, said you two were in the hospital for a good part of the evening."

I inwardly groan. Of course my mother thought it was appropriate to contact my boss. In her eyes, I am a 28-year-old toddler.

"It was nothing. Distal radius fracture, quick reset, cast for six weeks."

He nods solemnly. "Even still, you two will have to see patients together until that comes off, I'm afraid."

I turn around to check if there is another person in the tiny kitchen, anyone other than Lucas.

"What?!" we exclaim, equally disgusted by the idea.

"Dr. McCormick." I try to recover quickly. "I assure you, I don't need his help seeing patients. I'm perfectly capable of continuing on by myself."

To prove my point, I reach for the patient chart I brought into the kitchen and stuff it beneath my arm. I put my unopened granola bar between my teeth and then reach down for my empty mug with my free hand.

"Voila."

The granola bar slips out with the word and lands with a splack on top of Dr. McCormick's brown leather loafers.

He shakes his head and turns, not nearly as amused as he should be.

"Diane is waiting for you two in room four," Mariah says. "No rush. I just put her in and she's still getting her robe on."

Lucas and I look at one another and then book it out of the kitchen in tandem.

"Look, bike safety is not something to ignore," he says, pointing to my cast. "I think my parents still have

44

Madeleine's old training wheels in the garage. I'd be happy to install them for you."

I roll my eyes and let his words deflect off my bullshit force field. When all of this is over, it will be doubly satisfying knowing I out-doctored him with one arm tied behind my back.

"I can't believe we have to see patients together like we're first-year interns."

I elbow him out of the way so I can nab Diane's chart first. "Oh please. You should be so lucky to go into an exam room with me."

He nearly smiles and then covers it up with a hard cough. My heart soars and I cover it up with a cough of my own. We are two hacking doctors standing in the hallway, moments away from being locked in padded rooms.

"So how do we want to play this?" he interrupts, changing the subject and reaching down to angle the chart so he can read it as well.

"Let's alternate taking the lead," I suggest diplomatically. "I'll go first."

"Of course."

My time in the hospital waiting room the day before gave me a lot of time to consider my three-phase plan. Dr. McCormick went out of his way to lay down the criteria he's looking for: community engagement and patient satisfaction. The latter will come naturally, over weeks of working in the office and worming my way into our patients' hearts. The former will take some engineering, but I already have a brilliant idea.

Every year, Hamilton High hosts a fair that celebrates the founding of the town and gives kids of all ages an excuse to eat cotton candy until they puke. The PTA invites businesses to rent out booths and I plan on hosting one for

McCormick Family Practice. Community engagement: check.

"Dr. Bell, are you nearly finished reviewing her chart? I've never seen such medical devotion to a case of the sniffles," Lucas says, drawing me out of my thoughts.

I flip Diane's chart closed and open her door. "Ms. Pecos, how are you feeling today?"

"Terrible," she replies with a congested Texas accent.

"What seems to be the trouble?"

"Stuffy nose, watery eyes, you name it. I have a terrible headache that only goes away when I sleep. It's been this way for the last three days."

I check to confirm she has no fever.

"Ms. Pecos, we'll run a few tests to confirm, but it sounds like it could be a nasty cold. You might just have to let it run its course—"

"No! That won't work!" She wrings out her hands. "You see, there's this guy. We're supposed to be going on a *third* date tonight."

"Well if you're worried it might be contagious, you can always reschedu—"

"No, you don't get it. This is the sexiest guy I've ever dated, and I think he wants to take the relationship to the next level. *Tonight.*"

"I'm sorry, I don't—"

"I can't do...*that*...with a runny nose and puffy eyes!" She looks frantic.

"Well if he's a good guy," Lucas says. "He'll understand a little cold."

She looks between the two of us like we're idiots.

"No! Haven't either of you been with someone you're so attracted to you can hardly stand it?"

I swallow.

"Almost like you can't even handle standing in the same room as them. Your hands sweat, your heart rate goes up, and"—Lucas and I meet each other's eyes and then immediately glance away—"and I just want everything to be perfect. You have to help me."

I push Lucas closer.

"I understand. Don't worry Ms. Pecos, we're going to do everything we can to help. My assistant here is going to swab your throat so we can rule out a bacterial infection."

Lucas gives me annoyed side-eye, but still reaches for the long cotton swab.

Once he's swabbed her throat, he hands the sample off to Mariah in the hallway to prep. "How long have your eyes bothered you?" Lucas asks. "Were they irritated before you got sick?"

I hold my arm out to separate him from Ms. Pecos. "I apologize for the twenty questions—he's shadowing me today, and he's still learning how to interact with patients. Sit up straight for me and let's have a listen to your lungs."

I move around the exam table and maneuver into position, only to realize my cast will make it nearly impossible. I try to put my stethoscope on one-handed and Lucas steps closer.

"I don't need your help," I mutter.

He tilts his head and watches me struggle.

After ten long seconds, I get the stethoscope in place. "Right, okay. Deep breath for me."

I press my good hand to her back and try to maneuver the chestpiece with my casted hand. My attempt is futile.

Lucas grows impatient and steps closer so he can replace me. I don't budge, and there are suddenly too many cooks in the exam room.

"If you'd just step aside, Dr. Bell, I can listen to our

patient's lungs and rule out any pulmonary issues."

"I'm fine right here."

He reaches over, grabs my biceps, and shifts me out of the way like I'm filled with air.

I step right back to where I was before. He will not edge me out of this office. Ms. Pecos shifts uncomfortably.

"Dr. Bell, would you please join me in the hallway for a moment?" Lucas says in a measured voice. "I think Mariah might be back with the slide results."

He doesn't wait for me to reply, just walks to the door and holds it open like a parent who's caught me breaking curfew. I smile softly at Ms. Pecos and walk out, dejected.

When we're alone in the hall, he turns to me.

"What's your game plan, Daisy? We can't do this dance with every patient for the next six weeks."

"You are absolutely right. Here's a plan: you give your resignation and I go on with my life, happier than ever."

"You have one hand—"

"Lucas, you of all people should know how much can be accomplished with only one hand."

I flick my eyes down to his slacks—not because I care what lies beneath them, but because I need to shove the double entendre past his thick skull.

He steps closer, sustaining my taunt.

"You sound like you know from experience."

He's wearing a knowing smile and it's not the smile he wore as a teenager. That was easy to deflect. This little smirk holds dark promises and I realize suddenly that Lucas is a man now—a man who enjoys crowding my space and getting inside my head. I try to look past him, but his shoulders are too broad and he's waiting for a comeback so I open my mouth and speak.

"Um...Ms. Peni—MS. PECOS, I mean, needs us." I

clear my throat and look down the hall, praying for Mariah to round the corner. HOW LONG CAN IT TAKE TO READ THE TEST STRIP? She's nowhere, I am alone with Lucas, and the office is suddenly hotter than Hades. I pinch my lapel and air out my blouse. "I think we should…be doctors—stop looking at me like that. Just turn around while we wait for Mariah."

"You're blushing," he says, sounding pleased.

I've had enough; I turn on my heel to find Mariah and that godforsaken test strip.

She's in the lab and when she sees me, she tilts her head and her eyes assess me warily.

"Is everything all right, Dr. Bell?"

"Yes."

"You look really flushed."

"It's the A/C in this place. What's the thermostat set on?"

"62."

"Is that in Fahrenheit?"

"Do you want to sit do—why are you fanning yourself like that?"

She's handling me the way I handled the patients during my psych rotation, and sadly, she is smart to give me a wide berth.

It's day two and Lucas is already starting to unnerve me.

After the longest work day of my life, I stand on the curb, waiting for my mom to pick me up like I am back in the third grade.

"Yoohoo, paging Dr. Bell!"

HONK HONK.

My mom swerves in front of me like she's a soccer mom in a sporty hatchback commercial. For the next six weeks, she is my chauffeur. My cast has not only impeded my ability to see patients on my own, but has also forced me into vehicular dependency courtesy of my loud mother. There's no way I could ride my bike one-handed.

"Oh this is so fun! Just like when I used to pick you up early from school when you peed your pants or cried after visiting the zoo on a field trip. You wanted to set all those animals free." Her eyes glistened. "My little activist."

I squeeze my eyes closed and slide into the passenger seat.

"Mom," I hiss. "Please. Everyone can hear you—stop doing that—who are you waving at?"

"Look who it is!" She rolls down my window and shouts past me, "Lucas! Oh, oops! I should say, *Dr. Thatcher*!"

I don't turn to confirm that she is waving Lucas closer to the car.

"Dr. Lucas Thatcher!" she shouts and then says to me, "He has turned into *such* a handsome man."

I will not sit idly by while she compliments the uncomplimentable.

For half a moment we fight for control of the power window on my side. Up-down, up-down. I focus all the muscles in my body on the tiny button, but she thwarts me with a mother's most powerful tool: child lock. She pops them into place and slides the window down with ease.

"Evening, Mrs. Bell," Lucas says from somewhere on my right. I stare out the front window with a rigid focus. "For a second I thought one of Daisy's friends was picking her up. Is that a new haircut?"

My mom titters and touches her ends. "Oh stop it, you. It's nothing. Just a fresh trim."

"Mom, we had better get going. Traffic is getting pretty bad," I say, pointing out the front window.

"Nonsense! There's nothing on our schedule except leftovers and *Masterpiece Theater* and I haven't seen Lucas here in so long. Has it really been since…last Thanksgiving?"

I stayed in North Carolina for Thanksgiving last year and my mom subsequently regaled me with stories of how the Thatchers invited her over to their house for Thanksgiving dinner. She and Lucas allegedly played board games together "for hours".

Lucas leans down and props his elbows on the open window. "You're the reigning Pictionary champ. Those weekly painting classes have really been paying off Mrs. Bell."

"Oh, you know I only go to those for the wine."

My mother is flirting. I turn my back to Lucas so I'm facing the center console. "Mom. I'm tired and I'm hungry."

"Maybe now that the gang's all back in town, we can get everyone together for game night?" She pins me against the seat with her arm. Her ability to ignore me is baffling. It's a wonder I wasn't malnourished as a child.

I consider reaching down and punching the gas pedal with my casted claw-hand. There are several children crossing the street ahead of us, but it might still be worth it. She's got a clean driving record and no priors; with the right judge and good behavior, she'd be out of prison in no time.

"Seriously, Mom. I feel faint." I make my voice sound

wobbly and weak.

"There's half of a Fiber One bar in my purse. Listen, Lucas, you tell your mom I'll give her a call later this week and we'll set it up."

He agrees with a "yes ma'am".

Who is he kidding?

"I'll see you in the morning, Daisy," he says before tapping on the hood and walking in front of the car. Pedestrians on the sidewalk crane their necks to watch him like he's something special.

I roll my eyes.

"Rough day?"

"The roughest. You know, I don't see why you still talk to him. You're supposed to be on my side. You're my mom."

"I'd be on your side if you were right, but in this case, you're both in the wrong. You two have taken a silly childhood molehill and renamed it a mountain."

"You don't understand. Lucas is to me as Wanda Wade is to you. Remember when she bribed the judges with homegrown tomatoes and dethroned you from Hamilton Lawn of the Year from 2013-2015?"

"That is nothing like you and Lucas—Wanda Wade is just a cheating bitch. Lucas is so nice!"

This exchange is nothing new. Lucas and I both have two personas—one for when we are alone together, and one for when we are in public. That's why nobody on the outside ever truly understands what we represent to each other. I've tried countless times to show my mother the error of her ways when it comes to Lucas, but he brainwashed her years ago. I was alone in my hatred for Hamilton High's prom king, which was especially irksome because we were crowned together. Our senior class apparently thought it would be hilarious to see the two of us slow dance together under the neon lights set up in the basketball gym.

I can still remember the dumbfounded expressions on everyone's faces, watching the two mortal enemies of Hamilton High pressed together on the dance floor. I remember his hand shaking, enraged at the voters for forcing us together like that. I could feel his pulse through the palm of his hand.

"Did your mom fix your tie for you, or is that a clip-on?" I taunted.

"Just shut up and spin," he retorted, twirling me like a stupid ballerina.

"If you plan on dropping me during a dip, I'm taking you down with me."

Halfway into the song, I noticed him looking at my face, his eyes fixed in concentration, his expression tortured.

"Stop looking at me as if I somehow fixed the polls. Trust me, you are the last person I want to be up here dancing with," I seethed in response to his strange look.

He shook his head and broke away from me, having reached his limit.

The crowd around us erupted.

"A minute fifteen!" someone shouted, waving his watch in the air. "Who bet they wouldn't go over a minute and a half?! Come collect your money near the punch bowl!"

"Daisy." My mom shakes me out of my distant memory as we arrive home. "You have that same look on your face that you used to get in high school. Are you still thinking about Lucas?"

I close my eyes. "Not by choice."

R̶x

CHAPTER SIX

The next day, I need to get out of the house, so I volunteer to do the grocery store run for the week. Sure, driving with my clunky cast isn't all that easy, but I manage to pull into a wide space near the back of the parking lot just fine. I'm exhausted from work and could use a nice relaxing evening at home, but my mom is a hoverer, especially now that she thinks I'm damaged goods. Compared to enduring her claustrophobic nurturing, strolling through the grocery store to the crackly tones of Billy Joel's "Uptown Girl" will be like my own personal spa day.

It's not long before I realize my mistake. Back in North Carolina, I could typically go out without fear of running into a single person I knew. Here, in Hamilton, it's the exact opposite. I close my eyes and try to visualize how I must appear. I showered after work and pulled on a pair of sweats and a t-shirt. My hair is still damp and my face is makeup free. *Not your best look there, Daze.*

As if it's orchestrated by some cruel god, I'm stopped by no less than five people on my walk toward the sliding glass doors. It's mostly people welcoming me back or asking how my mom is doing, but I make a break for it when a neighbor asks me to look at a mole on her upper thigh.

Once inside I feel safer, but I snatch a People magazine from the rack for camouflage just in case. I'm multitasking, reading an interview about Ben Affleck while bagging zucchini when I see Lucas on the opposite side of the vegetable section. He's changed since work too. He's wearing workout clothes and a baseball hat. His glasses are gone and his t-shirt looks damp, as if he's come straight from the gym.

He looks up, sees me staring, and I whip the magazine up to cover my face.

Go away. Go away. Go away.

I'm repeating the words under my breath, hoping he'll disappear like a reverse Beetlejuice. Just in case my magic spell doesn't work, I turn my back toward him and stuff zucchinis into my cart like CNN has just announced a worldwide shortage.

I can only imagine his snide remark: *Big fan of zucchini?*

I stand there, shaking, wondering how long it will take him to come over and pick a fight, but after another minute or two, I look over my shoulder and realize he's gone. He didn't come over.

Huh.

I straighten my shoulders and finish weaving through the produce section with a sense of dread. Suddenly, the tall aisles feel like the walls of a maze, with Minotaur Lucas lurking somewhere within. I decide to skip the middle of the store and head straight toward the back wall of meats and cheeses, hoping to spot him before he sees me.

Ugh. He's two steps ahead, checking out the poultry. I know he sees me out of the corner of his eye, but he doesn't turn. He gathers an armful of lean chicken breasts, which

I'm sure his body will somehow transform into another row of abs. He continues on, always a few yards ahead of me. It's torture. I can't seem to care about spaghetti sauce when I know Lucas is on the opposite end of the aisle choosing between two brands of pasta.

Does he really not see me? What game is he playing?

I purposely linger a little too long in front of the chips—spoiler, Ben Affleck is probably going to get back together with Jennifer Garner. I'm hoping to lose Lucas for good, but it's no use. We meet up again in the frozen food section, passing right by each other. I brace myself, awaiting the remark he's taken all this time to craft, but nothing comes. He breezes right past me like we're strangers. I stop and turn over my shoulder. He's picking ice cream. Now I know he's faking—he's too in shape for desserts. In his workout clothes, I can see every inch of his broad chest and toned legs.

Before I know what I'm doing, I push my cart right up to his. With my cast on, though, I don't have much control over the trajectory, so I end up ramming it into his like a bumper car. It isn't an intentional use of force, but I sort of like the tone it sets.

"Hey there, Daisy," Lucas says. He's smirking, but his gaze stays pinned on the ice cream.

I bend forward, trying to meet his eyes. "Enough, Lucas. I know you've seen me shopping."

He tilts his head at the ice cream display. "Rocky Road or mint chocolate chip?"

This must be a mind game, but as a self-titled authority on ice cream, I can't not answer.

"Are you kidding? Rocky Road is gross. Who wants nuts in their ice cream?"

He reaches in and grabs the Rocky Road, plops it in his

cart, and turns his back to me. He's already halfway through the frozen pizzas by the time I realize he's blown me off.

Out of spite, I reach in for the mint chocolate chip.

I catch up to him in front of the milk. He wants 2% and so do I. He reaches in for a gallon and holds it up for my inspection. I nod and he puts it in my cart.

"Thanks."

His gaze falls over my cart as he heads toward the yogurt. "Did you leave any zucchini for anyone else?"

"Ha! I *knew* you would bring up the zucchini!"

I sound disproportionately pleased about this, like I'm an interrogating detective and my perp just confessed.

"I'm just curious about what you—or anyone—could possibly do with that much. It's filling up a quarter of your cart."

I hadn't thought that far ahead.

"Bread," I declare proudly, like a toddler that knows twelve words.

"Zucchini bread?"

He sounds like he doesn't believe it's a thing. By some miracle, it is.

"It's delicious. Like banana bread, but better."

He nods. "I'll take your word for it. Yogurt?"

"Greek."

"Same. Here, try strawberry-on-bottom. It's my favorite."

I don't protest because it's my favorite too. There are a few one-dollar-off coupons dangling from the shelf and I grab them all for myself, trying to provoke him out of this bizarre calm. Infuriatingly, he only smiles and heads toward the front.

"Are you done shopping?" he asks, casually plucking a

tube of Crest off an endcap.

I nod, mute.

We walk in silence toward the checkout lines. There's no one ahead of us, so we finish up at the same time. Seeing my cast, the teenaged bagger offers to help load up my car, but I decline. It's a slippery slope into old-ladydom, and I won't be taking my first step at 28.

Lucas isn't so easy to brush off. "It's going to take you an hour to load all those bags one-handed."

It's like we're right back at work—me at the mercy of my rival—but while I don't have the choice to refuse his help from 9-5, I do now.

"I'm okay. Really."

"Right, then you won't mind if I help."

My more dramatic brain cells tell me he just wants to get me alone in the back of the parking lot, stuff me into the trunk when no one's watching. In reality, he unloads the bags into my mom's car swiftly and then steps back, hands in the air like he's under arrest.

"That wasn't so bad, right?"

God, he's cute in the hazy light from the parking lot, almost boyish in his baseball hat.

"Torture," I muse.

He shakes his head and drops his gaze, smiling at the pavement a few feet in front of me. It's almost like he enjoys my cheekiness. I guess he would. After all this time, he has to enjoy our fighting as much as I do. Anyone else would have walked away a long time ago.

He starts to back away, over to where he's parked his cart by his truck. "For the record, you're the one who came up to me in there."

"*What?*"

"I know most women don't enjoy bumping into people

when they're out in their sweats. I was trying to do the polite thing—pretending not to see you."

"I thought you were trying to psych me out."

He laughs and turns, throwing his last few words over his shoulder. "Right, yeah. I guess it doesn't matter. I think you look pretty cute like that."

He means in my sweats and no-makeup state. I'm actually taken aback; even my dramatic brain cells think he sounds genuine. I'm left staring out after him, trying to decipher the last thirty minutes in my mind. It's only during my drive home that I catch sight of myself in the rearview mirror and scream. *No. No. Dear god no.* I forgot I was wearing stupid under-eye masks my mom wanted me to try. They've been stuck to my cheeks for the last hour. I look absolutely insane, like an over-moisturized raccoon.

That's why Lucas was giving me space. He was trying to save me from the embarrassment.

My mom assures me it's not as bad as it seems.

"On the plus side, your skin looks really great now."

I groan and stuff the carton of milk in the fridge.

"Also, Daisy…what the hell are we going to do with all this zucchini?"

℞
CHAPTER SEVEN

A lot of people used to wonder if my friendship with Madeleine was purely strategic, as if she existed only to be my eyes and ears behind enemy lines. Though I was sometimes tempted to use her as a spy, my love for Madeleine had nothing to do with the intel she provided me on her brother. Living next door to her for nearly two decades, she became the little sister I never had.

Madeleine was everything Lucas wasn't: friendly, decent, human. She was two years behind us in school, but I often forgot. She was wise beyond her years, and though I'd tried many times to turn her against her brother, she never picked sides. *He's really nice to me*, she said as I tried to enlist her help in procuring a voodoo doll. *Don't be so hard on him*, she insisted after I dreamt up a diabolical plan to get him deported.

After moving away from Hamilton for college, I weighed the pros and cons of continuing my friendship with Madeleine. She was indisputably my dearest and closest friend, but she was also my last remaining connection to Lucas—something I refused to hold against her.

In college, I could block Lucas on every social media

account and delete him from my phone, but if I wanted to maintain my relationship with Madeleine, I had to endure the occasional mention of him. The occasional mention turned into regular updates as I began to enjoy the ability to keep tabs on him from afar—all the juicy gossip with none of the personal investment.

"He's met someone," she said during one of our Skype calls in my second year of medical school.

"Another demon?"

"I think he really likes her."

"Watch out for a lobotomy scar, or the mark of the devil. It might be tucked beneath her hair."

"They're coming home at Christmas so he can introduce her to our parents."

"Hold a mirror up to her and see if she has a reflection."

A month later, Madeleine had informed me that Lucas had broken up with his girlfriend just before the holidays. Cold. Suddenly, I felt bad for the poor girl. She couldn't have known what a heartless monster he was when she signed up. He really ought to be on a government list.

It became a sort of game over the years with Madeleine. I acted bored and disinterested when Madeleine brought up Lucas, but not *so* annoyed that she would stop doing it. I could never, under any circumstances, bring him up first. Fortunately, I had become very good at this game of plausible deniability over the years.

"My mom wants to do a game night soon," I say, scooping out another bite of the brownie à la mode.

"Oh fun!" Madeleine agrees from across the booth. We are wrapping up dinner two days after my mother first suggested the idea of a game night to Lucas in the car.

"Yeah, personally, I'd rather sit through a root canal, or

maybe a spinal tap, but she's set on the idea, so I just wanted to get a quick headcount. So it'll be me, you, my mom, your parents, and Lucas. That makes six, right? Unless you or Lucas want to add a plus one? I just need to know how many extra chairs to pull out of the garage, and I was going to make a dozen cupcakes, which makes two for each person, unless..."

"You want to know if he's with someone, don't you?" She doesn't sound overly accusatory, just as if she's stating a fact. I suddenly realize I am not as good at this game as I thought.

"No, it's just that those chairs are super heavy..."

"Daisy, I know you better than anyone. I also understand the weird friction you have with my brother, so you don't have to worry about any judgement from me."

"Friction implies contact. What we have is magnetic repulsion."

"Well however you want to describe it, you don't have to worry. He hasn't dated anyone since his second year of residency, and he definitely has not shacked up with anyone since he got home."

I scoop another bite of brownie out of the bowl.

"You're smiling," she accuses.

"I'm not one of those people who derives joy from other people's sadness, but I can't help but love the idea of a sad, lonely Lucas."

"Well enjoy it while you can. Now that word has gotten around that he's back, I've been getting a suspicious number of calls from old friends and acquaintances. They pretend to want to catch up, but every conversation leads to Lucas and his relationship status." She narrows her eyes theatrically. "Not unlike *your* line of questioning just now..."

"Don't lump me in with those bottom feeders. I just want to get an accurate headcount for charades."

"Uh huh. You're pathetic. Can I have that bite?"

"It's the last one."

"How about you give it to me and I don't tell my brother you've been asking about him."

I hand her my spoon. "You're diabolical."

She grins. "Blackmail suits me. You two aren't the only ones to learn a few tricks over the years."

We finish off the dessert and debate whether our stomachs can suffer through another round.

"Count me out," I say, dropping my spoon and reclining in the booth. I am more chocolate than woman at this point.

"Same. Let's just finish our wine and then I'll drive you home."

I nod.

"I meant to ask earlier, have you been seeing anyone?" she asks.

"Madeleine."

"What? I'm just asking."

"As you know, I'm still building my Tinder profile. Once it's up and running, guys will be swiping so fast their thumbs will fall off."

"You've been trying to build that for the last year. It's two lines of text and a couple pictures, how hard can it be?"

"Oh Madeleine. You're still young and unlearned in the ways of love. There's an art to attraction."

"Yeah, put up a bikini picture and sit back while the guys start to sweat."

"If I wanted to find a guy who only values me for my bangin' bod, I'd just wear a bikini every day," I say sarcastically.

"You're right, you need pictures that show that you're

more than just a pretty face. Maybe pose with your white coat and list your name as Dr. Love."

Truthfully, dating isn't exactly my specialty. There seems to be no in-between with doctors fresh out of residency: they are either married with four kids, or they've missed the boat and remain totally and hopelessly single. I am in camp #2. Medical training has delayed my life. Because of it, I have a long history of half-baked relationships that never quite made it out of the oven.

Now it's time to focus on my love life again. At 28, I feel like I'm right in my prime. Mostly by accident, I'm in good shape despite having no time to workout. In residency, I couldn't stomach much of the hospital food. Coupled with frenetic sprints around the hospital and daily bike commutes, I maintained the illusion that I paid a modicum of attention to my physical fitness. Another bright spot for me is that men regularly mistake my exhausted ramblings and honest deprecation as humor and personality.

In conclusion, if dudes can look past the lime green cast and my impressive list of shortcomings (more added every day!), they'll see that I am one stone cold fox.

"I have an idea, but I know you won't like it," Madeleine says as she drives me home.

I shrug and look out the passenger window. "You're probably right. Don't tell me."

"There's this Hamilton Singles event next week—"

"Yep, that sounds like a fun journey to take all by yourself."

"Well...I've signed us both up for it."

"What a hilarious joke, Madeleine," I deadpan. "Maybe we should take you to an open mic night instead."

"It's next Wednesday and it starts at 7:00 PM."

"I'm so glad you feel comfortable enough to share these details with me, but they are irrelevant considering I won't be attending."

She pulls to a stop right in between her childhood home and mine. Madeleine doesn't live there anymore; she rents a small house just off Main Street, meaning our old walkie-talkies are out of range (I convinced her to try). As such, I'm the only one dipping into the past, staying in my childhood bedroom with my too-small bed trying to pretend that in the 11 years I've been away, I've actually grown up.

Madeleine insists I will be going with her next Wednesday and I put up a good fight. Truthfully, I already know I'll go because I hate to disappoint her, but I can't shake a scary thought that overwhelms me as I walk up the driveway.

By 28, I really should have things figured out. I should have built a well-rounded life for myself, but in actuality, I have been stuck in the same loop for nearly three decades. The backdrop has changed and supporting characters have flitted in and out, but the script has stayed the same: I am Daisy Bell, rival to Lucas Thatcher, and the weight of carrying around that hatred has started to wear on me. Deep down, I'm starting to forget what exactly it is I hate about Lucas. Right now, I can disguise it with logic. I want to own my own practice and I'm not good at sharing, therefore I want to run Lucas out of town. But, if it were that simple, I wouldn't have spent the last 11 years mentally throwing darts at his face. We were a country apart from one another, and I still gave him free room and board in my mind.

That leads me to believe this is a sickness I can't cure. At this point, my loathing for him has become a bodily function. Eat, drink, hate. When Lucas pops into my head, my stomach clenches and my heart pounds. I try to whack-a-mole thoughts of him out and my brain keeps putting in quarters. I even tried DIY therapy once: I put a rubber band on my wrist like a smoker trying to kick a pack-a-day habit, and every time Lucas popped into my head, I snapped the rubber band. By the end of the day, my swollen wrist was rubbed raw.

If the brakes have been cut and my hatred for him is in the driver's seat, my only hope is that this job with Dr. McCormick will cure me. I will complete all three phases of my diabolical plan and convince Dr. McCormick to name me his sole successor. Once that happens, I have every reason to believe my hatred for Lucas will be exorcised in one fell swoop.

Done. Finito. I will be free to write a new script. I will be Daisy Bell, gracious winner, beautiful taker-of-the-high-road. I won't rub his face in it or gloat. I will just forget about him.

Dear God, please let me forget about him.

R̶x̶

CHAPTER EIGHT

Lucas and I were once grouped as partners for a book report on *The Catcher in the Rye*. We both read the book and agreed to meet at the library (neutral territory) to work on our presentation. That ended up being the last thing we agreed on.

"Holden Caulfield is a spoiled hypocrite, and the only reason he's so bitter is because he's finally being called out on it," Lucas argued.

"He's just a kid!" I insisted. "All kids are immature to some degree, but that doesn't make his criticism of the adult world any less true. The adult world sucks."

"Oh, so it's everyone else's fault he's been expelled from every school he's attended?"

After an hour of debate, the giant poster board was cleaved down the middle. When it came time to present as a group, we considered divvying up the five-minute allotment, but neither of us wanted to give up the honor of going first. Instead, we both just talked over each other the whole time.

Seeing patients with him feels like a lot like that project.

"Could be an ear infection," I ponder.

"What about her loss of appetite?" Lucas argues.

"That's a symptom."

"I think it's best if we rule out separate intestinal issues as well."

"I don't think we need to run additional, expensive tests—"

"Um...excuse me?" Ms. Keller, our patient's mother, tries to get our attention, but we ignore her so we can continue our fight.

We justify the unprofessionalism because by all objective measures, patients are getting more time and double the expertise. In reality, it's overkill, and the subjective measures catch up to us quickly.

"Okay. Right, you two, I've been getting some feedback from your patients," Dr. McCormick says on Friday afternoon after our first week of working together.

I smile, prepared for praise.

"A few have complained of poor bedside manner, arguing over minutiae. I thought you two might set aside your old games when you're seeing patients, but it looks like I was wrong."

I am crestfallen; it's Lucas' fault. I don't hesitate before trying to push him under the bus. My mouth opens, but Lucas is quicker.

"I think we just had a few kinks to work out"—I bristle at his word choice—"but we have the hang of it now and come Monday, we won't let you down."

Dr. McCormick claps him on the shoulder, all buddy-buddy. "That's what I like to hear, son."

SON?!

"Can I still expect you on the course tomorrow?" he continues. "I want to try to get to all 18 holes before the sun gets too high."

Lucas flashes his winning smile, the one with the

dimples and the straight white teeth. I blink to shield myself from it.

"Looking forward to it, sir."

With a nod, Dr. McCormick turns back down the hall, and Lucas turns to me, smile still in place, though now it's a weapon.

"Don't worry, I'm not going to use this alone time with Dr. McCormick to lobby for your dismissal, but who knows? Maybe while we're having a few beers in the clubhouse, he'll come to that conclusion all on his own."

I narrow my eyes. "You're the worst."

"Sorry, did you think after all this time, I'd gone soft?"

It's a trick question, but his smile has slowed my response time. My gaze is halfway down his strong, *definitely not soft* frame when I realize what I'm doing and whip around.

"Have a good weekend, Daisy," he calls after me. He could not sound more pleased with himself.

Come Monday morning, Lucas is tanner than he was on Friday, which I know means he went golfing with Dr. McCormick. I wonder who won, but as I pass him in the hallway, I don't ask.

"Oh, Daisy," he says from behind me. "I left a little something on your desk."

I offer no response. I've yet to have an ounce of caffeine and my wit is sluggish this morning. Plus, I'm curious. Did he leave another bouquet of daisies? The scorecard from their round of golf?

Neither.

Sitting on the center of my keyboard is a 4x7 photo of Dr. McCormick and Lucas on the golf course, hip to hip like they are conjoined twins somehow separated by 30 years of age. Dr. McCormick is laughing and Lucas' eyes seem to follow me around the room.

Perfect. While he was schmoozing our boss with his long game, I was at home, in my pajamas, watching old movies with my mom and Madeleine.

I take a Sharpie from my drawer and suddenly Lucas is sporting devil horns and a tail. Defacing the photo doesn't get me any closer to winning, but as I pin the picture on the bulletin board beside my computer, I feel just a tiny bit better.

My first patient isn't due for another fifteen minutes, so I decide to do something I've dreamed about for the last week. It's pretty unethical, but technically not illegal—at least, I don't think it is. I bring up Indeed.com and search for open M.D. positions around the United States—the farther away from Hamilton, Texas, the better. *Oh look, Honolulu needs doctors.* With a simple drag and drop, I've submitted Lucas' CV, which I copied from the practice website. Just like that, my Monday is looking up. *Aloha, Lucas.*

Wednesday after work, my mom is shampooing my hair in the sink. With my cast on, it's easier to just to let her do it than to fight my mane one-handed. She'd scrub me down from head to toe if I let her. Mothers.

A few minutes ago she started going on about calling an exterminator out to the house soon, but I tune her out. I've got enough problems of my own.

"And well anyway, they said we'd have to vacate for a week or two while they put one of those big circus tents on the whole house! I'm not sure I'm going to do it yet. Oh look! It's Lucas—"

I jerk up and slam my forehead into the faucet.

My mom, bless her soul, doesn't laugh. "Ouch. You okay hon?"

"Fine."

I rub my forehead as I run to the window where she pointed, and it's true—Lucas is outside, mowing my mother's lawn in the buff. Well, he has low-slung workout shorts on, but no shirt, and I run back to the sink. I pretend I'm going to throw up from the sight of him.

"Surely that's against the deed restrictions," I say. "Aren't there decency laws?"

"It's Texas, Daisy. It's got to be 90 degrees out at least, who could blame the boy?"

She calls him a boy, but Lucas is all man.

"I'm going to go check the mail," I say.

I'm having what I can only assume is a hot flash. Maybe the sight of a glistening Lucas has caused me to tumble into early menopause.

My mom shouts after me, but I ignore her and yank the front door open.

Lucas is up to something. Mowing my mom's front lawn? He hasn't done that since we left for college, when she hired a service. The fact that he's doing it now, 11 years later, is absolutely absurd.

He pauses when he sees me strolling down the front path, but he doesn't say a word and neither do I. I stomp, stomp, stomp down to the mailbox, yank it open, find it empty, and slam it closed again.

When I glance over, sweat is rolling down Lucas' chest. *Dear god.* I'm still not convinced this isn't somehow illegal. I notice a group of female speedwalkers stopped on the street corner, gawking at Lucas. Oh really? All four of them needed to tie their shoes at the same time? It's called a double knot, people.

I wave my hand to shoo them away and they scurry off, embarrassed, but not really.

"You're causing a scene," I snap at Lucas. "Surely you can chop blades of grass while wearing clothing."

"I can put my shirt back on if it's a problem for you."

"It's not. For me. I don't care."

"Really—is that why you're checking the mailbox like that?"

I cross my arms. "What's that supposed to mean?"

"You've got shampoo in your hair."

That's when I feel the wet suds slipping down my cheeks and chest, soaking my tank top.

"It's leave-in conditioner."

"Fascinating."

"Daisy! Hun," my mom calls from the front stoop. "You already got the mail earlier. Now come on in and leave poor Lucas alone. I need to rinse your hair anyway."

Her ability to ruin a moment is uncanny.

"Oh, and Lucas," she continues. "I left some lemonade here for you in case you get thirsty."

"Satan doesn't get thirsty," I mutter under my breath as I drag my feet up the front path. The last thing I see is Lucas' reflection in the window: buff, sweaty, disarmingly handsome. That night, before I go to sleep, I retrieve the massive box fan from the garage, turn it on full blast, and aim it right at my bed. The hot flashes are getting worse.

Friday afternoon, Lucas and I are presented with Mr. and Mrs. Rogers. They're newlyweds in their late 40s with a penchant for PDA and an aptitude for over-sharing. They insist on a joint appointment and they sit on the exam table *together*, their hands linked. Their intake form mentioned painful rashes, but little else.

"You see…we went hiking on our honeymoon and well, you know how romantic it can be out in nature—"

Mr. Rogers blushes and pinches his wife's side. "T-M-I, Kathleen."

"They're doctors! They need to know the full story if they're going to help us, Mitch."

Lucas nods good-naturedly. "So you were hiking and then…"

"Well we're newlyweds," Mrs. Rogers continues, and they both flash their rings in unison. "Did we mention that? That we just got married? It's crazy. Mitch and I used to hate each other in school. He bullied me on the playground! Isn't that ridiculous? Well anyway, we bumped into each other at a bar, one thing led to another, and well—"

"I asked her to marry me on our first date. I knew she was the one for me, even back in elementary school."

I need to clear my throat, but I don't want to draw attention to myself. I know Lucas wants me to look at him so he can arch a brow and say, *Isn't that interesting*, but I resist.

"Let's get back on track. Where exactly were you hiking?"

My voice sounds weird.

"Out in Big Bend. We were camping there too."

"And things got a little heated on the trail?" I suggest, trying to connect the dots.

"It was Mitch's idea!" Kathleen giggles. "He swore no one would see, but then I think we got a little carried away…"

Fifteen minutes later, after a short exam, it's clear that Mr. and Mrs. Rogers are each sporting intense cases of poison ivy, concentrated around their nether regions. Yikes.

They leave with a prescription for extra-strength hydrocortisone cream and clear instructions to lay off sex until the rash subsides. I don't think they will. I smile and shake my head as I finish jotting down notes in Mrs. Rogers' chart. Lucas is beside me, leaning against the wall with his arms crossed.

"Aren't you going to finish Mr. Rogers' chart?" I ask, staring up at him from beneath my lashes.

"I did."

I look back down and start to write faster.

"So that's it, isn't it?" he asks.

"I have no idea what you're talking about."

I do, but I want him to drop it.

"You've had a crush on me this whole time, just like Mr. and Mrs. Rogers."

I bark out a laugh. It's forced and fake. "Don't you have something else to be doing? Like planning your next tee time with Dr. McCormick?"

"It's already on the schedule, and you're avoiding the question."

"That's because I'm trying to work," I say, writing the same word in Mrs. Rogers' chart for the fifth time. Thank god for white-out.

"That's fine. Your secret's safe with me."

It feels like he's coming on to me and it's hard to

believe that, in this old war, there are any unused weapons remaining in his arsenal, but this one is fresh off the line and my mind reels in its wake.

I narrow my eyes and try to decipher his motives, but his neutral expression betrays precious little. I don't know if he's a surgeon with a knife or a child with a rock—either way, he wants my jaw to drop and my heart to quicken, and I don't disappoint. My face is on fire. Whatever his intentions, he's found a new, hidden chink in my armor. Lucas and I have been at this for so long that he very rarely gets a rise out of me, an unexpected reaction. I turn on my heel and slam my office door closed, nervous for what his next move will be.

R.S. Grey

℞
_____

CHAPTER NINE

LUCAS

From: lucasthatcher@stanford.edu
To: daisybell@duke.edu
Subject: Unsent Email #349

This feels a little strange. I haven't written one of these messages in a while, not since before I moved back to Hamilton. Can I even call them *messages* if I never hit send? I'm not even sure you're using this email address anymore. Dr. McCormick keeps saying he'll give us new ones for the practice, but coming from a guy who still uses Windows 98, I wouldn't count on it happening any time soon.

I looked the other day, just out of curiosity, and the first time I wrote one of these...journal entries? Shouts into the void? Whatever I decide to call them, the first was during my freshman year at Stanford. It was a week into fall semester and I guess you could say I was homesick. At least that's what I told you in the email. I went on and on about missing Hamilton and I never once mentioned that I missed you.

I guess I'm pretty good at keeping secrets. I never told you I applied to Duke. I got in with a full-ride, same as you, but then I overheard your conversation with Madeleine before prom. You went on and on about how excited you were to move away. You couldn't wait to get out of Hamilton and get away from me.

I got the message. Loud and clear. It might've been the first time in our lives that one of us actually took a hint, ha.

I went to Stanford, ready for a fresh start, but instead I spent my entire freshman year thinking about transferring to Duke. I didn't join any clubs or make those lifelong friends that end up being your groomsmen. I hung out in my dorm room and listened to those CDs you used to make for Madeleine. (I stole most of her collection before I moved.) There was something comforting about listening to the songs you'd handpicked, even if they weren't for me.

God, that was a long time ago, a decade, and yet I can still remember being that eighteen-year-old kid away at college and so homesick it hurt.

I got over it—I got over a lot of things—but to this day I've been bothered by the one question it's too late to ask.

Would it have hurt more or less if I'd just sent that first email?

℞
CHAPTER TEN

This fight with Lucas is different than it used to be. 11 years ago, our weapons were conventional and agreed upon: report cards, race times, SAT scores, death glares. There were no innuendos or subtle hints of foreplay. I would have guessed that high school Lucas couldn't have differentiated between foreplay and his forearm. Adult Lucas can. It seems Stanford taught him more than biology. I should write a letter congratulating and admonishing the dean.

I don't have a problem with the war evolving.

It's that I have no clue what's lurking around the corner, what little tricks Lucas has stuffed up his sleeves today, and it's putting me on edge. It's making me second-guess every decision I make.

Monday morning, I slip into a black dress that hits my knees, stand in front of the mirror, and try to see myself from every angle. Yes, it looks appropriate from the front, but what if I have to dip down and retrieve a pencil. Will the seam ride up tastefully, or will it scream out *yee-haw*?!

I replace the black dress with pants and a blouse. No danger with fitted wool trousers.

Except these days, being around Lucas affects my

internal thermostat. I'm no longer able to regulate body temperature the way I'm accustomed to. I replace the wool pants with a thin pencil skirt and then leave my room before I toss another article of clothing onto the floor.

It has been two weeks since Lucas and I started working together at McCormick Family Practice. I've had enough time to adjust, and yet when I stroll into the office Monday morning and see him preparing a cup of coffee in the kitchen, the sight of him still shocks me.

There are milliseconds that pass in which I see Lucas as everyone else sees him—tall handsome doctor with thick brown hair and a perfect white smile—but it's a mirage, a fictional oasis that disappoints as I draw near and remember that the image belongs to Lucas Thatcher.

"Having a case of the Mondays?" he asks, suspicious of my inspection of him.

"Wouldn't you like to know." I sigh before urging my legs to propel me into the relative safety of my office.

Once I've dropped my things beside my desk, I open my purse and pull out the items I collected before leaving the house: a bottle of red nail polish Casey fawned over and a hardcover edition of *Dark Matter* for Gina. They're not bribes, per se, just gifts meant to elicit support—all part of Phase II.

After the book and nail polish are gratefully accepted, I float around in a triumphant haze. *Giving really can be better than receiving,* I think as Lucas and I walk into the exam room to see our first patient. Mrs. Vickers. 56. Ankle pain with slight swelling. I have the lead, but Lucas will undoubtedly cut in at some point to offer his own two cents. I want to smash his piggy bank.

"Mrs. Vickers, good morning. I'm Dr. Bell and I'll be taking care of you today."

"Jesus! Finally!" She slams her magazine down on the floor. I reach down to pick it up, but she doesn't want it back, so I clutch it awkwardly. "Where do you get off making people wait? I had an appointment at 7:45 AM and it's 8:00 AM. Do you think I can just sit here and wait on you all day? I have a job too, you know."

I want to correct her—our first appointments of the day are always at 8:00 AM—but I'm still drifting on a cotton candy cloud.

"I'm truly sorry about that," I say sweetly. "I understand your time is important, and I want to make this right. After you leave, go across to The Brew and tell them to put your coffee on Dr. Bell's tab."

"Ugh, coffee gives me diarrhea. Listen lady, you think that because you're wearing a white coat you get to rule over everyone else around you? Well guess what? I won't stand for it. You better believe I'm leaving a bad review on Yelp."

I can sense Lucas behind me, no doubt enjoying the attack. *Not so eager to jump in on* this *patient, are you Dr. Thatcher?*

"Mrs. Vickers, there's nothing I can do now except get you healed up so you don't have to waste any more time here, so let's get to the point: you mentioned some swelling and tenderness on your right ankle?"

Her arms are crossed and her eyes are narrowed. I can tell she was looking for more of an outburst to feed into her provocation, but I've disappointed her.

"Yes. The right one," she mumbles, turning away.

"Then let's take a look." I drop her chart and magazine on the counter and step forward. It's another five minutes of games before she lets me examine her foot. The bruising and sensitivity paired with her story of the tumble down the stairs definitely warrants concern.

"I think we ought to send you down to the county hospital for a weight-bearing x-ray. It's definitely sprained, but we need to rule out something worse."

"You can't do that here?! This is ridiculous!"

"I'm sorry. We're a small family practice clinic. We don't have the equipment—"

"Oh save your bullshit for someone else, Blondie. My Yelp review is only getting longer," she snarls, pulling out her rhinestone-encrusted smartphone.

"All right, that's enough." Lucas' voice booms from behind me and I go pin straight. "You're obviously having a bad day, but if you can't treat Dr. Bell with the same respect she's showing you, I think you should take your healthcare needs somewhere else. When you get there, I'd also suggest starting with a weight-bearing x-ray."

My eyes are so round with shock they must take up half of my face. For maybe the first time in her life, Mrs. Vickers is speechless; she is clearly more accustomed to bullying teenaged cashiers at Dillard's. She stares at Lucas in silence for a few seconds before she turns to me, not quite meeting my eyes. "Which hospital did you say?"

Lucas is back in the kitchen pouring his second cup of coffee when I walk by later that morning. I stop and turn to him, aware that we've already stood on these marks this morning: him with his coffee cup in hand and me lost for words.

From anyone else, I would have openly appreciated the show of support, but I don't want Lucas to see me as some damsel getting her first taste of distress. Being in medicine has exposed me to far more and far worse than Mrs. Vickers, and I've learned to handle it in my own way.

"Did you explain what happened to Dr. McCormick?

I'll corroborate your story if needed," he says, like I need an alibi in a murder investigation.

I shrug, trying hard to ignore the urge to thank him. "He wasn't surprised. She's apparently caused trouble here before. I don't think she'll be back."

"Good, and by the way…" His brows are furrowed and he's wearing a troubled expression. "I know you had it covered back there, but I couldn't just sit there and let her talk to you like that."

I tilt my head and study him. "So is that it? You're the only one allowed to bully me?"

Silence follows unlike any I've heard before. It's not the absence of sound, more like a held breath, or nervous words caught in a nervous throat.

He turns to me and for a few seconds we're locked in a staring contest. His brows furrow again and then I think, *He's beautiful*. The thought springs up out of nowhere and I try to shove it back in its box. Too bad it doesn't fit anymore. There's no use in trying to deny it. He stands there staring at me with chiseled features and punch-you-in-the-gut brown eyes. My breathing picks up and Lucas notices. He's staring at me like he wants something.

Like he wants *me*.

I tremble. I want him to answer my question so I can bolt into my office and barricade the door, but instead, he leaves his coffee and pushes off the counter. He steps into my personal space. It's an intimate approach, one with intent, and when I realize I'm backed against the wall, my heart rate attempts a Guinness world record. Hummingbirds have nothing on me.

I have to look up to see his face and even then, I don't see much. His features are indecipherable. Have I insulted him? Turned him on? I nearly laugh at the second option, but then his gaze flicks to my lips and I don't feel like laughing anymore.

He bends low and my stomach flips. For some incomprehensible reason, I wonder if he's going to kiss me. Right here, right now, after 28 years of this war. Maybe he realizes he doesn't stand a chance going up against me head to head so he's employing the other parts of his body, but he should know that the street he's pushing me down goes both ways, and all the swords he's playing with are double-edged. Sure, he's no longer the scrawny Lucas from a decade ago, but even with his new Body by Puberty^{TM}, he has to have calculated the risk in playing a game of sensual chicken with me.

I lean in close, trying to show him that proximity doesn't bother me. My body brushes his, and I suppress my revulsion—or is that lust? Either way, I am in it to win it. I will mash my face into his if I have to.

His body is pressed against mine and the hallway is noisy. Someone will round the corner and he will have to step back.

"I asked you a question," I say, and then I regret it. My voice is shaky.

Is this a part of our war?

He looms over me as he raises a hand to my throat. I think for one horrible second that he is going to strangle me, but his finger brushes across my collarbone instead. Gently. Painfully.

"If you come any closer, I'll scream," I warn.

"I don't think you will."

I squeeze my eyes closed, preparing for death, and instead his lips press against mine. I am still alive.

Maybe more than ever.

My hands reach up to push him away. After 28 years,

it's instinct. Self-preservation. To their credit, my hands do make it to his chest, but then my synapses must get crossed, because Lucas Thatcher is kissing me and I'm not pushing him away. Lucas Thatcher, bane of my waking life and lead role in my nightmares is kissing me, and my good hand is wrapped around the collar of his white coat and tugging him.

Hard.

Against me.

My brain hums at max capacity, but all my neurons are bumping into each other, trying to reason out this exchange. Can you kill someone with a kiss? I think that's what he's doing—slaying me with his mouth. He leans in and bites my lip, and it's not gentle. I know the only hope of retaliation is to overwork his brain as well. I slide my tongue past his lips and deepen the kiss.

Take that.

He lets out a husky groan and hauls me against the wall. I'm pinned by his hips and I'm vaguely aware that either the tile floor has ceased to exist, or I've been lifted off of it. He's got me right where he wants me and my body, obeying a lifetime of training, refuses to back down. My breasts feel heavy and full against his chest. Even my nipples reach for him. My panties need to be changed and I'm ashamed, but not ashamed enough to stop. Lucas pulls back for a second, dragging in a haggard breath, and I jump on him, bringing his mouth back to me.

I say when this is over.

His hand wraps around the base of my neck, twining in my loose strands. I shiver and he tightens his hold. God, he's a good kisser. Of course he is. There is nothing Lucas Thatcher doesn't excel at and I find myself appreciating just how adept he is at mouth-to-mouth combat.

Too good. He tilts my head. Grips my neck. Presses. Deepens the kiss until I'm panting. Until a heaviness settles between my legs and I feel him against my stomach. It's a shocking sensation, a hardness I'd never considered.

He tastes like a guilty pleasure, one that will undoubtedly sour once I'm alone again. We are enemies. Foes. And yet when Lucas takes my waist in his large hands and rolls his hips with mine, I feel like we're working together to build something. Mutually assured destruction.

"I've paged them three times."

I register Mariah's voice, but it seems far away, miles at least.

"Really? Let me go see if I can find them."

Now it's Dr. McCormick. He's rounding the corner into the hallway we've been using as our weapons testing facility and Lucas leaps back so quickly, I don't have time to get my footing. I collapse back onto the tile in a heaping pool of desire and useless limbs.

"Daisy? Why are you on the ground? Mariah's been paging you."

"She lost a button."

It's Lucas who offers the insane explanation.

My mouth is open. Red. Bruised. Most definitely incapable of communication.

Dr. McCormick, shockingly, doesn't question us. He's too swamped with patients to consider that every button on my white coat is accounted for and my hair is sticking up in every direction. "All right, well look for it later. You two have patients waiting."

He turns back and leaves us, and I look up at Lucas, expecting to find him wearing his signature I'm-so-pleased-with-myself smirk.

Instead, his eyes are dark brown pools. Heated.

His breaths are as audible as mine and his brows are knitted together, almost like he's angry. His lips are a flat line of confusion, and then I think, *I kissed those lips.*

Oh my dear god.

I kissed Lucas Thatcher.

Did the earth just quake?

He reaches down to help me up and I wish I had thought quicker and stood by myself. I'm not ready for him to touch me, not when I am still coiled like a spring under pressure. He keeps hold of my bicep until I'm steady. I stare down at his muscled forearm, studying the tight grip he has on me. It's sizzling.

Gently, he brushes a bit of dust off the back of my white coat and then steps back. He looks like he did ten minutes ago. Dr. Thatcher, M.D. Poised. Handsome. Terrible. Me? I am a poor excuse for a human being standing on shaky knees.

"To your earlier question: yes."

"What?" I ask, my voice raspy.

"I'm the only one," he says before walking away.

R℞

CHAPTER ELEVEN

Ever since our little hallway mishap, I've started having what we in the medical field call "intrusive thoughts" involving Lucas. They are referred to as such because they are unwelcome, typically of an inappropriate nature, and completely impossible to suppress. The fact that I'm having them about Lucas is especially distressing because, apart from one NyQuil-induced dream I had in eleventh grade, I can honestly say I've never thought about Lucas in that way.

I'm eating my lunch locked inside my shoebox of an office while I casually dispatch Lucas' CV to high-ranking hospitals around Alaska. After I've hit send on the fifth submission, I start to digest both my turkey sandwich and Lucas' motives for kissing me. I know he is trying to get inside my head. What was once a childish chess match has turned into an X-rated game of capture the flag, except our underwear are the flags. I'm seriously considering going commando for a few weeks, but I don't think that will dull the intrusive thoughts.

Lucas innocently filling a cup of water becomes Lucas turning and drizzling it down the front of my white coat.

Lucas politely bending down to retrieve my dropped

pen becomes Lucas on his hands and knees, begging for me.

Medical talk becomes dirty talk. Stethoscopes and blood pressure cuffs become sex toys.

By closing time on Tuesday, I want to tap out. I've gone 28 years without so much as a second glance at the dweeb I used to call "Lucas the Mucus", and in the matter of one morning, he's rattled me. I need to go home and exorcise whatever demon he's awoken in me. I need to Amazon Prime some sage and perform an ancient cleansing ritual under a full moon in the center of town. I need to Google how to erase a few hours from someone's memory so I can go back to the way I was B.K. (Before Kiss).

I am cracking and I want to flee, but I still have to talk to Dr. McCormick before I leave. I have a plan for community engagement (Phase II) that will knock his socks off. I've planned a time to talk to him alone, near the end of the workday, because I am a coward.

At 5:58 PM, I tug open my office door and look to the left to see if Lucas is still here. His office door is closed, but the sight does little to calm my nerves. I tiptoe out into the hallway—carefully sidestepping the spot where the *incident* happened—and then I knock on Dr. McCormick's door. He's transcribing notes into his ancient computer but welcomes me in with a mustached-smile and an exaggerated wave.

"Heading out for the day?"

"In a second." I smile and hold up another bag of cookies. "I wanted to give you these before you left."

His eyes light up at the perfect blend of cinnamon and sugar. "More snickerdoodles?"

"My mom's recipe," I gloat. "I told her I needed to butter you up, and she said she knew just the recipe."

I swear he blushes. "There's a reason that woman was the top fundraiser at the Hamilton High bake sale while you were in school. I think I've purchased every damn doodle she's ever baked."

Yes. I remember.

He tears open the bag as soon as I bring it within reach and I use the opportunity to launch into my well-rehearsed speech.

"So I've been thinking about what you said the other week, about community engagement, and well, I took the initiative and booked a booth at Hamilton Founder's Day Fair next Saturday. It's up at the high school. We can do free blood pressure and BMI checks, low-cost flu shots, that sort of thing."

He leans back in a chair so worn I fear it will keep tipping until he's on the ground. Somehow, it stops just before he's horizontal. He points at me with his half-eaten cookie and nods. "That's fantastic. Our office hasn't sponsored a booth like that in ages. It's just the sort of thing I was looking for." I beam, but then Dr. McCormick ruins my moment. "You'll both go."

"Oh." I shake my head vehemently. "That's not necessary. The fair really isn't all that big. I'm more than capable of manning the booth all on my own."

His gaze falls to my cast for only a brief moment, but it's still long enough to tell me he doesn't think I can manage the booth without Lucas' help. If I could, I would gnaw the cast off with my teeth just to prove my capability.

"Oh I know you can, but I think it's best if you both go," he repeats, closing the discussion. "I trust you'll give him all the details."

And like that, my genius idea is splintered in two. I saunter out, dejected at the thought of having to share the booth with Lucas. Even on the way home, the promise of fried chicken can't lift my spirits.

"I'll just eat a salad," I tell my mom.

She slams on the brakes and then threatens to drive me to the hospital for a checkup. I lie about having had a hearty lunch. Then, I zip my lips. I don't trust myself; I fear thoughts about Lucas will slip out without my approval. *I KISSED HIM*, I shout in my head. Fortunately, she doesn't push the issue. Even when she's shampooing my hair in the sink later, she steers the conversation toward fluff.

"Did Dr. McCormick like the cookies?"

"He loved them."

"Oh?"

She's fishing.

"He raved about them. I've never seen him so happy," I continue.

She glows, my exaggeration doing nothing to dilute the compliment.

"Mom, you're getting shampoo in my eyes."

"Oh! There—better?"

"No. Ow! Stop poking my eye with the towel."

This is how my week has gone. First, the intrusive thoughts. Then, Dr. McCormick forces me to share. Now, I'm treated to melted corneas. My flimsy rock bottoms just keep giving way to deeper, darker depths. While Lucas is walking on clouds, I am a hundred miles below the Earth's crust.

It isn't until Madeleine's call Wednesday afternoon that I'm reminded of the real rock bottom waiting for me. I am at a seafood buffet for a Hamilton Singles event. All you can eat, all you can meet. There is a bevy of both shrimp and men. So far, the former has held the lion's share of my attention.

"Any good prospects?" Madeleine asks.

"Personally, I'm enjoying the coconut-crusted. Oh, and the scampi."

"Human prospects, Daisy. Put the shrimp down, already."

"Look Madeleine, the way I see it, I *might* meet a great guy tonight, but these shrimp are a sure thing. Take that guy there, he's put away at least four plates. He's getting his money's worth."

"Well for one, you're a fifth of his size. Two, I think he's under the impression that this is a speed-eating event."

"Maybe we're soulmates," I croon. I am the heart-eyes emoji.

Madeleine has had enough of me. I know because she takes my plate and hands it off to a pimpled waiter with an exasperated sigh.

"There's a nice guy who's been asking about you. He's over by the soft-serve machine."

She nods in his direction and I get a wink and a smile from the lonely cowboy. Instead of a six-shooter, he's holding a child-sized sugar cone. It ruins the appeal.

"That's a little too much denim for me."

"He's good-looking! In some parts of the world they call that a Canadian tuxedo."

"Well in my part of the world they call it a virginity force field."

She tosses her hands in the air and gives up on me. Finally.

For the next thirty minutes, I'm left to sit next to the

speed-eating yin to my yang. We don't talk until I'm cutting into a slice of cheesecake. He's as old as my grandfather; if he was younger, we'd already have eloped. I look over for his name.

"Where's your nametag?" I ask, finally aware that this man might have sneaked into the event.

"My what?"

"Are you here for the singles thing?" I ask, pointing to the herd of grazing singles I want nothing to do with.

"Singles what?"

He's hard of hearing, but I'm not discouraged.

"Yeah, me neither. You gonna finish that?"

He nearly forks my hand as I try to steal a bite of his brownie. He isn't one for sharing desserts. I respect that.

"That a friend of yours?" he asks, pointing a pudgy finger out past the front of the restaurant.

I glance up and come face to face with my worst nightmare.

Lucas is standing on the other side of the smudged glass, looking like the cat that caught the canary. He holds the Hamilton Singles event poster in one hand and my dignity in the other.

"He looks awful happy to see you."

"That's because he is," I groan, sliding down in my seat until I'm completely under the table.

Ŗ

CHAPTER TWELVE

LUCAS

From: lucasthatcher@stanford.edu
To: daisybell@duke.edu
Subject: Unsent Email #350

You probably think I'm happy I spotted you at that singles event, and you're right, I am—but not for the reasons you'd guess. I was smiling because from the looks of it, you'd managed to find the only man in the entire room that wasn't interested in you.

Thanks for that.

I think I'll sleep a little easier tonight knowing you didn't go home with anyone, knowing there's still a chance.

Then again, maybe I should give you hell for being there in the first place. I mean, c'mon. A *singles event?* You don't need any help in that department. Every guy in town has been asking about you since we got back.

I've tried to deter them, but pretty soon, one of

them is going to work up enough courage to do something about it.

I guess I'll have to beat them to it.

R̽x

CHAPTER THIRTEEN

"Well if it isn't Daisy Bell, the most eligible bachelorette in Hamilton County."

"Oh! And look, it's Lucas Thatcher, the only human man with no heart."

It's the morning after the singles event and Lucas follows me into the lab. We're supposed to be examining a slide, looking for an infection; instead he is examining me, looking for a weakness.

"You know, I can help with your situation if you need me to. Just say the word."

"First of all, I don't have a *situation*, and the only words I have for you are inappropriate for the workplace."

He comes up behind me as I'm looking in the microscope and brushes my loose hair off my neck. I freeze because there's nothing else to do. My brain is mush.

His breath hits the top of my spine. His fingers are on my pulse. I shiver.

"I'd be lying if I said I hadn't thought about it over the years."

I dig my elbow into his ribs, but it's not enough. I should have jammed the heel of my hand into his nose—a self-defense move I've always dreamed of trying on Lucas.

"This is an unwanted sexual advance."

I sound like a bored HR manager giving a presentation.

"So report me."

"Did you two look at the slide yet?" Dr. McCormick's jolly voice ricochets through the halls and Lucas steps back, finally.

"Yes sir. Her white cell count is high and Lucas just propositioned me for sex."

The second half is retained in my head.

"All right then. Let's get her on some antibiotics."

He walks off and I turn back to Lucas. He's wearing a smirk I want to steal.

"I reported you in my head," I tell him.

"I did something in my head too."

My cheeks burn with embarrassment. He's had the upper hand for far too long. The kiss in the hallway, him seeing me at the singles event, and now him teasing me in the lab has made me desperate. Phase III is behind schedule, but I can't tell him that.

I turn to the exam room across the hall and yank the patient's chart out of the cubby. I feel Lucas' eyes reading over my shoulder and try my best to tilt it in a way that inconveniences him. It's the only retaliation I can muster.

This setup is getting to me. With my cast, there is no way I can see my patients alone. Our proximity gives me no chance to regroup or strategize. He's winning and he knows it. It's time to take back the upper hand.

When Lucas happens to have the upper hand, he tends to gloat, and I've found that I can use this overconfidence to my advantage. The difficulty is knowing when an opportunity presents itself to flip the script. So, like a vengeful boy scout, I come prepared.

The next morning, I arrive to work twenty minutes before the rest of the office with a duffel bag full of ammunition. I brew coffee—the hazelnut blend, Lucas' secret guilty pleasure. Once the aroma has saturated the hallway, I go into my office, unzip the bag, and extract five things: a tray of lemon poppy seed muffins, a sexy workout outfit, a stopwatch, and two Rubik's Cubes. My plan is as follows:

After the last patient leaves, I'll microwave the homemade muffins so that they're soft and warm. Some people might have put laxatives in them—not me. I just made them extra fucking delicious. While they're nuking, I'll shimmy into my tight tank top and spandex shorts. I don't know if Lucas has a heart, but thanks to a fateful pantsing incident in middle school, I know he is a man. The microwave will *ding*. Lucas will take those first few bites (he cannot resist lemon poppy seed), and then I will stroll out as if I'm on my way to the gym.

"Are those Rubik's Cubes?" he'll ask.

I'll act surprised by his sudden interest in little ol' me.

"Oh, you mean these? I found them on the sidewalk this morning. I've never seen them before in my life."

"That makes sense," he'll say, swallowing the lies hidden in my Trojan horse of baked goods. "And what's with the getup?"

He'll pretend to be disinterested, but his Adam's apple will bob and he will steal quick glances down my body. He'll realize too late that I'm watching him, and when he urges his eyes back up to meet mine, I'll slowly tug on the dark lanyard hanging around my neck and extract a retro stopwatch from my cleavage. Finally, I'll toss him a cube.

"I was just about to go donate these to an afterschool program for at-risk youth, but before I do, care for a quick game?" I'll ask sweetly.

By game I'll mean contest—not that it'll be much of one. The moment I finish that Rubik's Cube before him, he'll be the one on the ropes. Nothing unsettles Lucas more than losing. Balance will be restored.

The sound of the office's back door breaks me out of my daydream and panic momentarily sets in before I hear Dr. McCormick's office door creak. There's still time to gather myself before I see Lucas.

Still, I don't get it together.

I almost give away my intentions all morning. My diabolical plan seeps from my pores.

"You are way too cheerful, even for a Friday," Lucas tells me when we're going over the chart for our first patient. "Did your friend from the dating event finally call?"

The need to participate in the real world snaps me out of my villainous scheming. "Lucas, you do realize that the only thing sadder than being at a small-town dating event is lurking around outside of one, right?"

My rebuttal gets him off my back for a little while, but he's still suspicious.

"You're smirking again," he says just before lunch.

"Am I?"

"Yes. Like the Cheshire cat."

Just then, Mariah comes around the corner. For the last week I've plied her with smiles, frappucinos, and the promise of a raise as soon as I take over for Dr. McCormick. She fits snugly in my pocket.

"The patient in room two is ready to see you, Dr. Bell."

She beams.

"Perfect," I reply with an appreciative smile. "Thank you, Mariah."

I tap, tap on the door for exam room two and walk in, leaving Lucas in my wake.

I know my happiness is throwing him for a loop—his Type A brain short-circuits at the thought of juicy information being kept from him. All afternoon, I get to enjoy how worked up my silence gets him. He won't stop flicking his eyes over to me during the exams. I can feel him guessing at what I might be hiding and trying to uncover my motives with his eyes. My mysterious smiles are a warning shot. As he sees his final patient, I prepare the uppercut by heating the muffins and slipping into spandex. I hum a little tune as I do it. I'm shaking with excitement. The image of his face when I beat him at the Rubik's Cube will sedate me for days, if not weeks.

"Dr. Bell?"

It's Mariah again, on the other side of my office door, hesitant to enter.

"Come in!" I nearly sing the words like a Disney character. If I knew lyrical choreography, I'd break into it.

"Woah! Dr. B..."

When I glance over my shoulder, Mariah stands in the doorway, eyes wide at my getup. After ten seconds, her heterosexual eyes have still not left my cleavage. Lucas will pee himself.

"What's up?"

Her mouth hangs open. She closes it and shakes her head. "Dr. Thatcher needs your help—"

On cue, a loud wail sounds through the office. Lucas' last patient was a pediatrics case: a six-month-old due for a round of shots.

"He's in with Mrs. Heckmann and her little baby. He asked for you to come, quick."

Could this day get any better?

My heart flutters and I yank the now useless stopwatch from around my neck. Mariah might as well have announced that Christmas came early.

You see, since the very dawn of our strife, we've each adhered to a solitary unspoken rule: never ask the other for help. Got sick, missed school, and need a copy of the day's notes? I would walk for miles to another classmate before calling next door. Bloody nose right as the curtains go up at the school play? I didn't care if Lucas was the president of a tissue factory, I'd have bled out before asking for one. So, if Lucas is truly calling in a lifeline, I won't need muffins or Rubik's Cubes anymore. I've already won.

The wailing is getting louder, and I don't have time to change. I yank my white coat off the back of the door and drape it over my workout attire. The white coat extends a foot past my short-shorts and I'm aware how pornographic the effect is. I am suddenly Dr. Sexy, right off the rack at the Halloween superstore. I smile to myself.

Mariah leads me to exam room one and the door is open, beckoning me in. There's a fretting mom sitting up on the table, holding her child in her lap. Her worry lines are so deep, she doesn't even notice my inappropriate garb. I explain it anyway.

"Mrs. Heckmann, I was heading to the gym when I heard the commotion," I say with a sugary smile. "Dr. Thatcher, need my help?"

Lucas turns over his shoulder at the sound of my voice and like a cartoon, his tongue rolls out to carpet my entrance into the exam room. It's an involuntary, caveman reaction, one he overrides almost immediately. I almost feel badly, as if I'm cheating. His jaw locks tight and his large hands turn to fists.

I know what he needs me to do, but I wait for him to say it anyway. I wouldn't want to presume.

"I'm having trouble with these shots."

And, I say with my eyes.

"And I think the patient might be more comfortable if you do them."

I walk up to the metal tray he has set up in front of his lap. I could move it, but where's the fun in that? My spandex-clad ass is less than a foot away from his face. He could roll his chair away, but I guess there's no fun in that either.

"What's her name?" I ask, mining vast deposits of untapped motherly mojo.

"Ava," Mrs. Heckmann replies shyly as I pop the lid off the first syringe. Lucas has already loaded the shots for me, so all I have to do is a little sleight of hand.

"How pretty!" I turn to Mrs. Heckmann. "Is it a family name?"

During my pediatric rotation years ago, I learned the trick in administering shots to babies is to distract both the child and the mother. Lucas probably neglects the second part. If mom is tense, the baby is tense, and the positive feedback loop gets ugly.

I talk, make faces, play peekaboo, and perform a magic act that starts with a handful of shots and ends with a smiling, inoculated baby.

"Thank you so much," Mrs. Heckmann says, staring up at me from the exam table like I am the messiah come to set her people free. She tries to spare Lucas' feelings. "Sometimes she gets nervous around men."

When we're back out in the hall, Lucas strips off his

thick-framed glasses. He is no longer the mild-mannered Clark Kent, but intimidating and evil.

In my head, I tell him to chin up before patting him on his white coat, right over the Lucas Thatcher, M.D. embroidery. I tell him, *I'm more than happy to help you any time you need it.*

In real life, Lucas tails me back to my office. His arms are crossed in my doorway and I feel like a caged animal with him blocking my exit. He is too big for his own good—poor Ava probably thought he was a bear. He never used to work out in high school, staying long and lean from cross country. Now he is tall and made of brick. The big bad wolf could not blow him down.

I hesitate before stripping off my white coat. I want to put my blouse and pencil skirt back on over my workout clothes, but I've gained too much ground to retreat now.

"You're good with kids," he says, and in the warmth of my victory, I foolishly take the bait.

"You sound surprised."

"I guess I shouldn't be—their innocent minds are probably easier for you to manipulate."

"Ha ha, Lucas. Is that why your mind is so hard to crack into? Lack of innocence?"

He doesn't reply, but he doesn't leave either. I pull my tennis shoes out of my duffel bag, notice the Rubik's Cubes, and feel like a fool. He never would have fallen for my ploy. Heat floods my cheeks, and I keep my head down as I tie my shoes.

The air is tense. I don't want to brush past him, but I can't stand his eyes on me any longer. With a bored sigh, I stand to leave and toss my duffel bag over my shoulder. Just as I think I'll make it out, he blocks my progress with his body. He smells like he just showered in the wilderness and dried off with freshly laundered woodland creatures; I detect pine and sandalwood.

His nose is no slouch either. "Are those lemon poppy seed muffins in the kitchen?"

I stare straight ahead, smack dab at his chest. "They're for book club."

"Oh yeah?" He doesn't believe me. I've never been a group kind of girl and he knows it. "What are you reading?"

To call his bluff, I tilt my head and lock eyes with him. "*A Game of Thrones*. You remind me a lot of Joffrey."

He smirks and I blink to mentally photograph it for later.

Still, he doesn't let me pass; I'm starting to sweat and I think he knows it. He knows the ball is back in my court, but he still wants to play.

"Make way, Dr. Thatcher."

His face dips down and his lips nearly brush my cheek. "Have fun at book club, Dr. Bell."

I shiver and shove past him.

On my way home, I pass a group of kids playing soccer behind an old church. I feel strange pulling up in a car and offering them free treats, but it's worth it to watch them greedily devour the muffins meant for Lucas. After all, it's not every day you beat Lucas Thatcher *and* nourish local youth. I brush my hands together in a job-well-done motion, sending stray poppy seeds cascading to the floorboards.

℞
_____

CHAPTER FOURTEEN

Madeleine invites me to her house later that night to make up for the shitty singles night she dragged me to. I accept her offer because even though I would like to stay angry with her, I already know from decades of experience that I will cave in a few days. I don't possess the willpower for long-term grudges. Besides, it isn't like my social calendar is exactly bursting at the seams.

I am instructed to dress up a bit because there might be other guests in attendance; I guess she's scared I'll wear a matching pajama set and embarrass her in front of her new friends. Who they are, I have no idea. Madeleine and I have been each other's only real friends for upwards of twenty years. We're like antisocial butterflies that never made it out of the cocoon.

Except when I arrive at her house on Friday, I am shocked to find not only a few extra guests at "movie night", but a slew of cars lining her street and blocking her driveway. I park one block over and hoof it back to her house, trying to pinpoint where the heavy bass is coming from. My first instinct is to assume Madeleine's house has been broken into. The perps, upon arrival, decided to stay and get cozy, make themselves at home, and throw a party.

It's much more likely than Madeleine Thatcher throwing a full-on frat house rager.

I'm halfway up the path with 9-1-1 pre-dialed on my phone when the door opens and my best friend appears in the doorway. She's wearing a tight blue dress that compliments her slender frame and light brown hair. She is stunning and giggly—I'd even go so far as to say drunk.

"DAISY! You're here!" She then proceeds to shout over her shoulder, "HEY EVERYONE DAISY IS HERE!"

"Everyone" cheers as if they know who I am, and when I walk through the door, I'm shocked, because they actually do. This is a high school reunion if I've ever seen one.

I wave, trying my best smile on for size, and then turn and yank Madeleine into the kitchen.

"You could have warned me!" I hiss.

"What? Why?! You look cute!"

I'm wearing my favorite jeans and a cream sweater. *Obviously* I look cute; that's not what I meant.

"You told me this was a movie night."

She laughs and reaches around me for an open bottle of Fireball. "Movie night schmovie night. This is your real welcome home party! Now here. Toss back a shot with me and loosen that scowl. You'll get wrinkles."

I don't want to accept the whisky from Madeleine because she's forcing it on me, but I sling back one shot, and then another. If I'm going to go back into that living room and converse with people I haven't seen since high school, I need to be under the influence. Like an adult.

My buzz sets in quickly since I haven't had a real dinner yet; I was planning on stuffing my face with popcorn while we watched movies. Clearly, that is no longer an option.

Madeleine parades me around the room making fake

trumpet noises, ensuring that every single person in attendance knows I've arrived. I try to catalogue the changes in my mind: who looks different than they did in high school, whose ring fingers are now bling fingers. Most everyone looks about the same as I remember.

The party has extended into the backyard where some guys have set up makeshift beer pong tables, and I even find myself intrigued by a stranger with his back turned to me. We'll call him NiceAss. Mr. Tall NiceAss. Madeleine hands me my third and final shot, I down it, and I point to him like I'm calling dibs. *That one.* The sting from the whisky still lingers as I saunter toward Mr. TN (for short). I'm prepared to lay on the charm when suddenly he turns and I catch sight of something other than his derriere. His profile stops me dead in my tracks. I'm sickened by the surprise.

Lucas?!

Madeleine is tittering behind me, more than pleased with herself.

Lucas turns to look over his shoulder, sees me. I half-wave with my casted hand. He frowns, clearly not pleased to see me, but I am pleased to see him—thanks to the whisky. It's the only way I can explain away how I feel about his amply filled navy blue pants and white button-up. He wore the ensemble to work, but with the sleeves rolled to his elbows, he's transitioned into play mode...and maybe I have too.

I consider berating Madeleine for inviting Lucas, but I know her response will involve cries of sibling guilt. She's chock full of it. Me? I count myself lucky to be an only child. No nasty older brothers to drag me down.

"Having fun Lucas?" I ask, interrupting the game of beer pong he was playing with our old classmate, Jimmy

Mathers.

Jimmy pauses mid-shot. "Oh hey, Daisy. Happy homecoming."

Neither of them seem very happy to see me, but I don't let that ruin my fun.

"How about I play winner?"

Jimmy laughs. "Well considering Lucas is about to beat me for the second time in a row, I'll just concede. The game is yours."

Lucas reaches for his beer and shakes his head. "Don't think it's a good idea. Why don't you go back inside?"

I bawk like a chicken, earning me a few laughs from the party guests lingering outside.

Lucas wipes his mouth with the back of his hand and there is an itty bitty smile there. I just know it.

"Fine. Grab a few beers, Jimmy. Daisy must be thirsty."

For the record, I have never in my life played a game of beer pong. My college days were spent at the library, studying, but it wouldn't be the first time competition with Lucas has forced me to be a quick learner. In the summer before junior year of high school, I condensed three years of Spanish into three months after finding out he took secret lessons to beef up his college applications. *Lo siento, Lucasito.*

Lucas sets up ten red Solo Cups in a triangle in front of me, and I nod with approval.

"Very good formation. My preferred arrangement."

"Do you even know the rules?"

I laugh. "*Pfft. Pah. Do I know the rules*? Enough about the rules, sissy boy. Let's get started."

I feel lucky that my cast is on my non-dominant hand, but I am fooling no one. By my third turn, I haven't even managed to sink a ball within a foot of the table. Lucas, meanwhile, has sunk almost every one of his shots, forcing me to drink the tepid beer in the cups.

"You can forfeit whenever you want," he says, his eyes rife with mischief.

"I would rather jump off a million bridges."

Those are the words my brain tells my mouth to say, but there is a distinct slur that accompanies them that even I notice. He probably hears something like *I drather pump my britches.*

"Let's make this a half game," Lucas says, eyeing my empty cups. "First person to five."

He's being a tricky-trickster but I see right through him.

"You don't think I can actually beat you," I say, taking aim for my next shot. I try a different tactic, closing one eye and trying to line up the trajectory of my ball using only the sound of the wind. I throw and the ball flies over Lucas' head...and hits Jimmy Mathers right above his ear.

"HEY! Watch it!"

"Ha!" I clap. "I play by East Coast rules. If you hit the last loser in the head, you automatically win."

"Nice try. You do realize the objective of the game is to get the ball inside the cups, right?"

He takes his turn and then I down another few ounces of beer.

"Okay I think that's pretty much game. Did you eat dinner tonight?"

"Yep. I had a sexy date. He bought me lots of fancy food. Let me eat it off his abs."

Another one of my balls goes flying across the backyard. Note to self: Spanish is easier to learn than beer pong.

I start to regret challenging Lucas, but then a loud crash sounds from inside, bailing me out. The music stops and someone is shouting about calling 9-1-1, about needing a doctor.

"I'm a doctor!" I shout, dashing inside to save the day. I envision performing a tracheotomy with a ballpoint pen or stitching up mortal wounds with craft string.

I'm disappointed to find that a guest was cutting limes for drinks when they nicked their finger. Another person saw the blood and passed out. I try to wrap my head around both things, but my vision is a bit fuzzy and I can't remember what day it is.

"Okay. Can someone repeat that to me? Slower this time?"

Lucas sidles past me. "Hey Mary Anne, let's get that finger cleaned up so I can see if you need stiches."

Just like that, he takes control. Confident. Strong. Relatively sober. Mary Anne stares up at Lucas like he's just proposed coitus. He guides her to the kitchen sink and runs water over her finger. She winces—it's either pain or an orgasm.

"Thank god he's here, right?"

I hear someone whisper those words behind me and I want to barf.

"Just another second," Lucas promises, tilting her hand to get a better view of the damage. "It looks like more blood than it really is. You'll be fine."

"That's close to the joint. You probably want stitches, Mary Anne."

That is my advice. I'm a healthcare professional so she has to take it.

Lucas disagrees. "A Band-Aid and some antibiotic cream ought to do the trick."

I throw up my hands. Mary Anne would probably take Lucas' advice even if he suggested amputation at the elbow. Where is that other patient? The head case?

She's lying on the couch, nursing her head with an ice pack. I pick up her feet and sit down.

"How ya feelin'?"

"Aren't you a doctor?"

I grin. "Bingo."

"Well I think I have a concussion or something."

I've been trained for this scenario. Head traumas were routine during my rotation in emergency medicine—though if I'm being honest, I treated those cases with significantly less alcohol in my system. I tell that to my patient.

"Great," she says, sarcastically. "You're wasted. I want Lucas."

I roll my eyes. "Nonsense. Now follow my finger."

She does.

"How many do you see?" I ask.

"Just the one?" she offers skeptically.

I *boop* her on the nose with the same finger. "You got it!"

A shadow falls over me and my patient's eyes widen. "Lucas! *Finally*. I was hoping to get a, uh…second opinion on my head. I fainted when I saw Mary Anne's cut."

He waves off her concern. "It's probably just a little bump. Get somebody to drive you home. If you feel confused or have a headache that won't go away, you might want to go see a doctor."

She frowns, clearly disappointed that she won't be getting her own mini exam courtesy of Lucas the Mucus.

I stand, annoyed that everyone considers him the medical authority. "No, go ahead, Lucas. She wants you to touch her. Feel her up."

"I hit my head!" she insists. Oh, *now* she's being coy.

"Daisy, can I speak with you for a second?"

Lucas tries to steer me out of the living room and away from the other party guests, but I'm not having it. At least, I try to jerk away from him, but he seems to have superhuman strength, and in the end, he very easily guides me where he wants—out onto the front porch.

"Are you okay?" he asks, hands on my shoulders, head dipped down so he can meet my eyes.

I grin. "*Bien.*"

"Daisy, drop the act. Nobody's around. You need food and water, and time to sober up."

I see right through his guise. "Am I the third patient now? You've seen the head case and the finger cut, now you need to check on poor drunk Daisy."

He lets go of my shoulders and yanks his hands through his hair. "I can take you home if you want me to."

I laugh like he's just proposed a date. "No thank you."

His eyes narrow and I'm reminded of Mr. Tall NiceAss. Suddenly I have the urge to lean forward and tell Lucas that even though he's still in his work clothes and his hair is all mussed up thanks to his hands, he is shockingly handsome for a nemesis.

I really think I'll tell him. My mouth is open and my casted hand is pressed to his chest so I can lean in and whisper the words, but the front door is yanked open and Madeleine is there. I pull back and wobble on my feet.

"I've been looking for you guys everywhere!" she says, oblivious. "Lucas, Mary Anne is asking about you, and Daisy! C'mon, I'm making a Chick-fil-A run."

She drags me down the path to her car and I look back at Lucas, watching us leave. He looks strangely sad standing beneath the porch light all alone. I have half a mind to shout back at him and remind him about the fair in the morning, but then I remember that I didn't want him there…didn't, as in now I do, but that's inaccurate. I don't want him there. My hatred for him is alive and well.

It has to be.

℞
CHAPTER FIFTEEN

The decision to wear cutoff denim shorts and a pair of red cowboy boots to the fair is purely strategic; I don't want to stand out like a sore-thumb-city-slicker in my smart-casual khakis. My lime green cast cannot be helped, but my mom curled my hair and suddenly, I'm Jessica Simpson circa 2001. I know I've done well when I arrive at the fairgrounds and garner a few second glances from the FFA cowboys. Yes, boys, these boots are *definitely* made for walking.

I'm confident my booth will be a hit. Sure, I'm still slightly hungover from the night before, and sure, the fair organizers have stuck me in no man's land between a deep-fried Twinkie stall and an elderly woman hawking bedazzled dream catchers, but I won't let that hinder me. After I tell Dr. McCormick that hundreds, nay, *thousands* of people lined up to get their blood pressure checked by *moi*, he will shower me with praise before looking ruefully at Lucas. *What has he done for me lately?*

I brought props with me: a small poster outlining the importance of heart health I peeled off an exam room wall and some branded pens I found in the bottom of the storage closet. They are dusty and the ink has dried out in most of them, but they're better than nothing.

The scent of freshly fried Twinkies wafts over and for a second I doubt myself. There are already a dozen people in line for them, and they have yet to give my booth even a cursory glance. There's a slight chance I overestimated fairgoers' enthusiasm for preventive medicine. A corner of my heart health poster comes loose and curls down.

And then I see him, just as I turn to fix the sign: Lucas Thatcher.

What the hell is he doing here so early?

The note I left for him specifically said: *Booth 1933, 6:00 PM*

But there is no booth 1933 and the fair ends at five o'clock.

"Good morning," he says, pleased with himself for disarming my trap.

"Lucas." I nod, assessing him. "Glad you could make it."

His black baseball hat and matching t-shirt are both printed with the McCormick Family Practice logo. He looks like an A-list hollywood actor we paid to be the spokesperson for our practice. On his shoulders rest two heavy duffel bags. He drops them on the table and my pens get pushed to the side.

"Easy, jeez. Are those bodies?"

"No, but this booth does look like a morgue."

He looks at the dozen scattered pens like they're trash. Then, he zips open the first duffel bag and starts to load our booth up with real swag—the good, expensive stuff. Adorable mugs that say "Keep Hamilton Healthy" in a scrolling designer font. Extra baseball hats. Fitted t-shirts.

"A few local businesses agreed to sponsor raffle prizes," he says, pulling out a roll of raffle tickets. "To enter, fairgoers just have to get their blood pressure or BMI checked with us. They're going to announce it on the loudspeaker."

It's a brilliant idea, but I don't tell him so.

"Yeah, well you're cluttering the booth with all this stuff, so if you could just—"

"Oh those mugs are so cute!" the elderly dreamcatching gypsy cuts in.

I want to tell her to mind her own booth, but Lucas is quicker. He takes one of the mugs and hands it over to her. "Thanks. If you have time later, we're doing free blood pressure checks."

She smiles at him with adoration and cradles the mug to her chest like she'll cherish it forever. My breakfast threatens to make a second appearance.

In a matter of minutes, my booth has been taken over by Lucas. It's now colorful and inviting. We've already had four people stop to enter the raffle and the fair hasn't officially started.

"I brought an extra t-shirt for you," Lucas says, holding it out. It looks to be my exact size.

I yank it out of his hand and after I've changed, we're transformed into two matching, smiling doctors. We're soon to be the most popular booth at the fair, but for reasons neither of us could have imagined.

"Lucas Thatcher and Daisy Bell?!" One of our classmates stops and stares between us. "Is this real? Are you two actually working together? Hey BARB! You aren't going to believe this."

Barb does not believe it, but when she sees it, she does tell Amanda who tells Sam who tells Ryan. Soon, word has spread throughout the Hamilton Founder's Day Fair. Though I'd assumed Lucas' raffle would attract the most people to our booth, in the end, people line up to gawk at the greatest side show of all time: Daisy Bell and Lucas Thatcher manning a booth together without coming to fisticuffs. To so many, it's unimaginable.

"So you and Daisy, huh?" Ben, another classmate, asks while Lucas positions the blood pressure cuff on his arm.

"What?" Lucas asks.

"Are you two really together? You two couldn't even get through high school algebra without Mr. Lopper seating y'all across the room from one another."

"We're working together," Lucas corrects. "And I'd like to think we've matured since then."

I meet Ben's eyes over Lucas' shoulder and shake my head. "We haven't," I mouth.

By lunch, we're out of raffle tickets and my hand hurts from puffing up the blood pressure cuff. Thankfully, the barbecue cook-off started a few minutes ago, finally driving attention away from our booth.

I sit down and yank my stethoscope from around my neck.

Lucas takes the seat beside me.

I can smell smoked brisket and my mouth waters.

"Hungry?" he asks.

It's the first bit of normal conversation he's directed at me and I'm too scared to look at him. The intrusive thoughts haven't diminished—they've grown worse. On Tuesday, he kissed me. On Wednesday, he spotted me at a singles event. On Thursday, he toyed with me in the lab. On Friday, he caged me inside my office and I almost came onto him at Madeleine's party. I am breaking the pattern. Saturday will be different. I am going to take those intrusive thoughts and bury them six feet under.

"Not going to talk to me?"

I shrug.

He ignores my silent treatment. "How was book club?"

I can't resist any longer. I turn to him and he's staring down at the spot where my denim shorts have ridden to my upper thigh. His eyes are the color of toasted walnuts today, dark, just like they were after our kiss. I heed their warning and stand, leaving Lucas to man the ship alone.

It feels good to put distance between us. Each step I take away from him gives me hope. Control. I wander through the barbecue cook-off, using the crowd to shield myself from the unsettling truths trying to stuff themselves into my brain. Did I give Lucas the wrong information about the booth so I wouldn't have to share credit, or was it because I knew I couldn't trust myself to be around him? At one point, I even found myself watching Lucas while he tended to a curvy brunette, wondering if he thought she was pretty. I was so perturbed by the sight that I didn't register the fact that my old classmate Beau's fingers had turned blue from how hard I'd inflated the blood pressure cuff on his arm. Right, well, his fingers were probably blue *before* he came to our booth.

I walk around the fair. Twice. I eat a barbecue sandwich and then double back and stand in line again to get one for Lucas. I'm two people away from ordering when I realize what I'm doing and bolt. I do not care about Lucas' hunger.

When I finally make it back to our booth, I've been gone for too long—Lucas is packing up his stethoscope and blood pressure cuff.

"Where are you going?"

Was I really gone all afternoon? I look up and the sun is still high in the sky. He's bolting early.

"Talking to me again?" he says, tossing me a knowing smile.

I hate when he does that. *Smiles.*

"Are you leaving?"

I realize I've stepped closer and am gripping the handle of his bag to rip it out of his hand and make him stay. I let go and step back.

When I speak again, I ensure my voice is even and normal. "I mean, it's fine if you are. I was just wondering."

He shakes his head and stands. "I got a call from Dr. McCormick. He needs me to go up to the clinic."

"What for?"

"One of his close friends is headed there. James Holder. Remember the guy that came in with flu symptoms last Monday? Apparently it's gotten pretty bad."

"Well I'm going with you."

"You can't."

I roll my eyes. "Like hell I can't. You're not going to go save the day and leave me here. Besides, half the people whose blood pressure we take end up going to the Twinkie stand anyway. I think we're losing the battle."

"Fine. We can ride over together."

My mom dropped me off at the fair and the clinic is over a mile away. I consider declining, but I won't give him the satisfaction of thinking he makes me uncomfortable.

"Yeah, fine. Whatever."

I tell Lucas to hold the duffel bag open at the end of the table, and then dramatically sweep the leftover swag inside. My cheap pens end up in the trash when Lucas isn't looking.

His truck is old, black like his soul, and in need of a major facelift. I'm surprised he's kept it all these years. His parents gave it to him when he was sixteen and he used to spend time fixing it up when we were in high school. I give the clunker a fifty-fifty chance of making it to the clinic without breaking down.

I open the passenger side door and stare inside. It has one long bench seat filled with items that belong to Lucas: an extra stethoscope, running shoes, workout clothes folded neatly on the passenger seat. Lucas moves them, but when I hop up and take a seat, I'm engulfed by him. His scent. With a spine-tingling shiver, I realize I am in his lair.

He starts the truck and buckles up. I try to do the same, but the buckle gets caught.

"It's broken. Here, let me." He unbuckles and reaches over to help me. One second I had a whole bench seat of separation and now Lucas is here, right on top of me. His hard chest brushes mine and suddenly I'm aware of every nerve ending in my body crackling to life. His mouth is inches from mine and because I don't trust my body, I zip my lips and press myself so hard against the seat that my skin fuses with the old cloth fibers. My good hand is fisted at my side.

"You have to sort of twist it and then tug real hard," he explains.

Are we talking about the seat belt?

"Daisy?"

I closed my eyes at some point, so I pry them open and he's there, hovering over me with a half-baked smile.

"You're blushing again."

He thinks he knows something, and I can't have that.

"I was just recalling all the dates you drove around in this truck back in high school." He squints and I like how the tables have turned, so I continue. "In cross country, Jessica Mayweather used to go on and on about what you two would do in this truck. Hope you got these seats deep cleaned at some point, Lucas."

He yanks my seat belt hard and buckles me in. It's too tight, but I don't struggle.

"She was exaggerating."

I turn toward the window so he can't see my smile.

We don't talk the entire way to the clinic. It's a gift considering I still can't quite wrap my head around the fact that I'm sitting in his truck after all these years. I wasn't even lying earlier. Jessica Mayweather did run her mouth every day, bragging about her escapades with Lucas. In total, they were together a couple weeks our junior year. In my head, it was years.

"I didn't realize you knew so much about my love life back in high school," he goads once we're on Main Street.

Well it's not like I had my own to focus on or anything...

I shrug. "Girls talk."

"Guys talk too."

"Oh yeah?"

He whips his truck into a spot in front of the clinic. "Yeah, I think I recall Bobby Jenkins going on about how much of a struggle it was to even get to second base with you. Said you were really stiff."

My cheeks have second-degree burns. If I ever see Bobby Jenkins again, I will sink a dagger in his heart. Now who's stiff?

An expensive blue sportscar pulls into the space beside ours and I recognize James Holder, our patient, behind the steering wheel. Without another word about my teenage bedroom skills, Lucas and I switch into doctor mode. I wrap my stethoscope around my neck and hop out of the truck. By the time Lucas has the front door unlocked, Mr. Holder is shuffling inside, looking ten times worse than he did two weeks ago.

"Mr. Holder?" Lucas asks, hurrying to help carry some of Mr. Holder's weight. With Lucas' help, we get him into an exam room. I retrieve his chart from the reception area and join Lucas in the room.

"It's gotten worse since I first came in," he explains. "I'm not eating, and on the off chance I'm even able to fall asleep, I wake up almost immediately, drenched in sweat. The rest of the time I'm just coughing up bloody mucus. This must be some flu."

A flu diagnosis made sense at the time: it's influenza season, he's older, and he's on medication that weakens his immune system. Because he was Dr. McCormick's personal friend, we decided to play it safe and send off a phlegm sample for culture.

"Daisy," Lucas starts, "I know it's Saturday, but can you try calling the lab to see if they have the results yet?"

Now is not the time to argue about who should be on administrative duty. I stride out to Gina's desk and call the diagnostic lab's number. After a handful of rings, I am prompted to leave a message, which doesn't help us at all. I step back into the exam room.

Lucas is checking his heart and lungs. "Deep breath for me."

Mr. Holder complies and I start asking questions.

"Have you changed your diet or medications recently?"

"No."

"Have you been overseas recently?"

"No."

"Have you ever had symptoms this bad before?"

"No, but it's the damnedest thing. The only time I've seen anyone cough like this was when I visited a slum in India. We went on a mission trip with the church, and I'll never forget the hacking some of those poor people dealt with from all that pollution."

My eyes widen, and I flip through his chart. "I thought you said you hadn't traveled recently?"

"Well that was over two years ago! Do you also want to know what I ate the day Reagan got shot?" He tries to laugh, but it only triggers a coughing fit.

"On this mission trip, did you come into close contact with anybody that looked like they were sick?" I ask.

"Hell, they all looked pretty bad. They were the untouchables. We were there washing their feet, handing out Bibl—"

His sentence is interrupted by a particularly ragged cough, and when he brings his hands away from his mouth, they're flecked with blood.

I cast a worried gaze at Lucas and shake my head. We need to step away from Mr. Holder. Now. My instincts tell me we're dealing with something much worse than the flu. I find two face masks in the supply cabinet and hand one to Lucas. I expect him to argue, but he puts it on and then turns to ensure mine is covering my mouth properly.

We step back into the room and Mr. Holder is leaning over with his head in his hands, clearly exhausted. Without a lab diagnosis or chest x-ray, there's not much more we can do. We gather what information we can: his temperature, blood pressure, and where exactly he was traveling in India, all clues to a diagnosis.

Once we've performed every test our small clinic allows, we tell him to sit tight as we walk into the exam room across the hall to talk in private.

"I think we're both thinking the same thing. Should we send him to county? There's only so much we can do here."

I agree, but try the lab's phone number one last time.

"Goddamnit," I exclaim, slamming the phone down

onto the receiver after another fruitless call. I close my eyes in frustration and when I reopen them, I notice the small red LED blinking on the answering machine. Gina usually checks the weekend messages first thing on Monday, but I hit play on the off chance it will help us.

"Dr. McCormick, Billy's got chicken po—"

I hit next.

"Can you get me in on Monday? I need a refill—"

Next.

"The cows got out of the pasture again, I need to resche—"

Next.

"Hello? This is Erika with Mission Labs. It is extremely important that you return this call as soon as possible. We received a positive culture for M. tuberculosis for a patient J. Holder and this individual needs to be placed in isolation immediately. Anyone in close contact should be monitored as well. If we don't hear back first thing Monday morning, we are legally obligated to alert the CDC."

"Lucas!" I shout. "DO NOT GO BACK INSIDE THAT EXAM ROOM!"

R̶x

CHAPTER SIXTEEN

"This is somehow your fault."

"Oh really?" Lucas replies. "Please, tell me how it is my fault that our evangelical, immunocompromised patient traveled to India over two years ago, before I even knew him."

"I'm still holding you accountable."

Lucas rolls his eyes and collapses back on the exam table: our little bed for at least the next 24 hours.

The CDC was quick—probably still jumpy after the recent ebola scare that swept the nation. They had four public health officials at our office within the hour. Two of them escorted Mr. Holder out into a waiting ambulance and two of them stayed behind with us. I suspected they wanted to gather the patient's history and ask a few questions, but it wasn't until I saw their overkill hazmat suits that the idea of a full-blown quarantine became apparent.

The officials gently guided Lucas and me into an exam room and told us to stay put. They promised they'd return in a few minutes and we believed them...just like Mr. Holder had believed us. Quicker than I could have imagined, they had red tape unraveling and our door locked from the outside. I panicked.

"Hey, wait!" I shouted, pounding on the door to get their attention.

"Ma'am, please calm down. We're transferring Mr. Holder to an isolation facility in Houston for treatment."

"That's wonderful," I said, shaking the doorknob to get out of the room. "So we can go?"

"Not so quick." The official held up his gloved hand. "I've got good news and I've got bad news. The bad news is that because you were in such close contact with the patient, we need the two of you to remain here in quarantine until we're sure you didn't contract the infection. The good news is that if your skin tests are negative after 24 hours, you'll be free to go."

24 hours? How could being locked in an exam room with Lucas possibly qualify as good news?

"Right. Okay. And so you're only going to keep Dr. Thatcher here since he was the one to touch Mr. Holder, and I get to stay at home on a mandatory vacation? Sounds reasonable. If you just pull that red tape back a bit, I can slip right out."

They stared blankly without indulging my hysterics.

"Just be glad it's only a day. Because you first saw Mr. Holder two weeks ago, any infection would have had time to become detectable."

He told us all of this an hour ago and since then, I haven't given up hope of escaping. Lucas has. He's lying on the exam table with his arm thrown over his eyes. I think he's asleep.

My escape will have to be an individual effort.

"Hey, psst, buddy. Pal."

I tap on the glass window on the exam room door and try to earn the attention of the official posted up right outside. He is my jailor and I have a plan.

132

"I know you can hear me out there. Do you have a name?"

He doesn't move. His last job must have been with the Queen's Guard.

"Listen, I'll have you know that I am a *very* sexy doctor, with a *robust*...immune system." My voice has taken on a slight edge of hysteria, but I hope it comes off as seductive. "If you let me out of here, I'll unzip that vinyl suit, rip off that mask, and show you just how uninfected I am."

The suggestion doesn't tempt him, so I try a more obvious approach.

"Oops. My top just fell off. I'm naked right behind this glass window. Sooooo naked. Naked as the day I was born—but sexier."

"Daisy, he has headphones in," Lucas says from behind me.

I scowl. "How do you know?"

"I saw them."

Somehow that is the last straw for me. I turn from the window and start pacing the small exam room. "Are you kidding me?! We're stuck in this room with nothing to entertain us and he's out there listening to a podcast?"

"Could be an audiobook..."

He is amused.

He is stuck in this room with me for the next 24 hours and he is wearing a little smirk and reclining on the exam table like he is on a beach in Ibiza.

"Wait." A panic-inducing thought spirals through me. "How are we going to survive for 24 hours without food?"

"They gave us food."

He points to a small Tupperware on the counter and I go over to inspect it. There are a few granola bars. Bottles of water. MREs. I keep rifling through our rations until I come up with a chocolate chip cookie they must have dropped in to keep morale up. I slip it into my pocket when I'm sure Lucas has closed his eyes again.

I look around the room and the walls seem to have contracted an imperceptible amount. I spy the small bathroom attached to the exam room and shudder.

"You mean I have to pee with you five feet away? Are you kidding me?"

"Or you could hold it."

A small, pitiful noise comes from the back of my throat.

"Are you losing it? Because if you are, you should let me know so I can restrain you."

I shoot him a glare. "I'd like to see you try."

Movement out in the hallway distracts me and I leap toward the door. "Hey! Yoohoo!"

The official has pulled a chair over to the door so he can sit down, and I've grown desperate—so desperate, in fact, that I shout through the door that I am starting to exhibit symptoms of TB. It's a lie, I hope.

"You know what?" I cough-cough like Karen from *Mean Girls*. "I have chest pain, chills, and a fever. I think you'd better take me to Houston too."

He finally turns to face me.

"Oh thank god!"

I can taste freedom. He will let me out. He has to listen—I am a doctor after all. When the tests come back negative, we'll all laugh and I'll be on my way with the chocolate chip cookie still stuffed in my front pocket. Lucas will be back here eating cold survival porridge.

"She's lying. She just wants out," Lucas warns, bored. He's found a stress ball somewhere in the room and is throwing it up over his head and catching it. Over and over and over.

"Lying?" I shout, all too aware that I've exceeded the volume of an inside voice. "I'm not lying!"

The official shakes his head; he's sick of my shit. He turns the volume up on his iPhone and I catch a glimpse of his audiobook: *Harry Potter and the Prisoner of Azkaban*. It's ironic, and I can't help but feel a kinship with Sirius Black—except instead of being locked away with thousands of soul-sucking dementors, I've only got one, and he's currently staring at me.

"You might as well relax," he says. "We're not getting out of here before our skin tests are negative."

He's still tossing around that damn stress ball, and I've reached my limit. Without hesitation, I storm across the room and snatch it out of his hands. In a feat of superhuman strength, I rip it down the middle. Tiny pieces of foam float down around us; for a few seconds, we live inside a shitty snow globe.

"Well, you've officially lost your mind," Lucas says.

"How much longer do we have?"

He checks his watch. "22 hours and 35 minutes."

I won't survive it.

"Lucas."

"Yes?"

"I think you should restrain me now."

HOUR 2

To distract me from my crumbling sense of sanity, Lucas agrees to do a quick inventory of the room. We have the following items to entertain us for the next 22 hours:

- 5 *Highlights* magazines, 3 of which have already had

their differences spotted
- 1 Sharpie, 1 pen
- 6 boxes of gloves, 87 tongue depressors, 55 Q-tips, and 164 cotton swabs
- 1 box of paper drapes
- 7 one-size-fits-all gowns
- CDC-issued blankets and cot
- a bunch of other medical supplies that don't help me forget that I'm a prisoner

"Well, there is only one logical way we're going to survive this," I say, gathering up the 87 tongue depressors and getting to my feet.

Lucas eyes me curiously. I stand at the door and put one foot in front of the other until I have the room mapped out. 120 square feet divided by two leaves each of us with 60 square feet to call our own. Of course one person will get the exam table, but the other person will get access to the bathroom, so our two autonomous nations will have to institute some form of trade.

"What are you doing?" he asks.

I nudge him with my foot. He's in the middle of my tongue depressor divider line.

"Giving us a border. It worked for Korea, it can work for us."

My tongue depressor DMZ doesn't keep him out of my side for long.

"Hey, you have to formally ask if you want to come into my space."

"You kept the food on your side."

That wasn't an accident.

He rifles through our stores and then settles on an apple. For the next ten minutes, I listen to him crunching on it with my teeth gritted.

"How can you be so resigned to this?"

He assesses me over his half-eaten apple. "Have you ever thought that maybe I don't mind being stuck in here with you?"

I laugh. "Hilarious."

He shrugs and bites off another piece of apple. He's either practiced his straight face in a mirror or he wasn't being sarcastic just then. None of my training has prepared me for option two.

"Listen, enough with the therapy. I have one last idea for how we can get out of here."

He doesn't humor me with a response, but I continue anyway.

"If you hoist me up, I can reach those panels in the ceiling. I'll pop one off and climb out through the air ducts. When I find the time, I'll come back for you."

He finishes his apple and tosses the core into the trashcan on my side. I'm still waiting for him to reply when he heads into the bathroom to wash his hands in the sink. He pats them dry slowly and then walks back out, leans against the exam table, and crosses his arms. His eyes meet mine. He tilts his head and he studies me. I sweat under his gaze.

"Why do you want to get out of here so badly?"

I frown. "Isn't that obvious? Who wants to be stuck in quarantine for 24 hours?"

"No, you don't want to be in here *with me*. Why?"

"If you don't know by now, after all of our history—"

"I think you want me to kiss you again."

My mouth drops open and words slip out like stones plopping into water. "Me? Want. You. Want. Kiss? Again? HA."

Shockingly, he doesn't understand my new dialect of English.

"It's just a theory," he says, then calmly changes the subject. "Let's play a little game: truth or dare."

"We don't have time for games."

This is the first time that comeback doesn't apply. We have nothing but time. I sigh.

"Fine." I roll my eyes at having to indulge him. "Dare."

"Let's start slow. I dare you to give me that chocolate chip cookie you stuffed in your pocket earlier."

How many eyes does he have?!

"No!" I pat my pocket to ensure it's still tucked away safely. It's my tiny sliver of hope in an otherwise bleak existence, and to keep it, I have to change my choice. "*Fine*. Truth."

He smirks, pleased. "Have you fantasized about our kiss in the hallway?"

℞

CHAPTER SEVENTEEN

Lucas is making a real show of eating the cookie I surrendered. It's filled with those big chocolate chunk pieces and I'm sure he doesn't even appreciate them.

He shoves the second half back into the cellophane wrap. "I think I'll save the rest for later."

"Or you could give it to me."

He arches a brow. "Oh? Are you ready to answer the question?"

"Not so fast, asshole. It's your turn. Truth or dare?"

"Dare."

My imagination runs wild with the possibilities. *The chance to force Lucas Thatcher do anything I want him to.* I can't screw this up.

"I dare you...to..." My eyes wander to the bathroom door.

"I'm not licking the toilet, Daisy."

"Ugh, fine. I command you to give me the other half of that cookie."

He seems disappointed as he hands it over, and I try to guess at what he was hoping my dare would be. Something funny? Something sexy?

HOUR 3

"What are you doing?" he asks.

"What everyone does in these situations—I'm turning inanimate objects into friends. Tom Hanks had Wilson, and I have Gary."

I hold up the blue nitrile glove I craftily stuffed with cotton balls. With a Sharpie, I drew Gary a face.

Lucas smiles for a fraction of a second before turning and shaking his head.

"We saw that," Gary and I say.

HOUR 6

Lucas is napping and I'm going through his things. I'm not normally a snoop, but I'm so bored. I was counting the freckles on my arm when I looked up and noticed the pile of his things sitting on the counter. Car keys. Stray coins. Wallet.

The wallet was too tempting to pass up.

The leather is smooth and worn; I guess he's had it forever. All the sleeves and pockets are full, and I take my time going through each one, checking over my shoulder every few seconds. He's still asleep on the cot.

There's a little bit of cash, a few stray business cards, a punch card from Hamilton Brew. All very typical. I pull out his driver's license and silently laugh at the old photo. Comparing the Lucas in the photo with the one asleep in the corner, I can admire how the features I once ignored have been etched and sharpened by time. I try to shove the card back behind the vinyl sleeve, but something blocks it from sliding in smoothly: a small, folded piece of paper. I tug it out and realize it's a photo.

The faded lines from the picture's creases don't dull the shock of recognition. It's one of my school photos. Seventh grade. The worst school photo I've ever taken. Even now, I cringe. Let me describe it: my blonde hair is frizzy and wild. I sport large eyes, desperate for the rest of my face to catch up. My freckles feature prominently across my nose and cheeks. Braces have turned me into metal mouth and my eyebrows are out...of...control.

I thought I'd confiscated and burned every copy of this photo, but apparently Lucas got his hands on one. He's probably saving it for my funeral, where he'll have it enlarged and propped up with daisies beside my casket. I'm half-tempted to rip it into a million tiny shreds, but I don't want him knowing I rifled through his things.

I hear rustling behind me and replace the photo and his license with superhuman speed. The wallet is right where I found it when I hear his feet hit the ground.

"What are you doing?"

I don't turn around.

"Nothing."

My voice says differently.

He laughs wistfully. "Do you even know what it feels like to tell the truth anymore?"

Truth: have you fantasized about our kiss in the hallway?

He walks over and yanks his stuff off the counter. My gaze is pinned on the floor. "That's what I thought."

HOUR 7

I wake up from a short nap on the exam table and inhale the sharp scent of fumes—permanent marker fumes. When I reach up to wipe sleep from my eyes, the smell gets worse, and then a devastating sight comes into view: my entire cast is *covered*.

"LUCAS!"

I sit up and see him sitting on the stool in the corner, rearranging the items in his wallet.

"LUCAS!" I shout again. He still doesn't look up. He pulls an old business card from his wallet and tosses it in the trash.

"I can't believe you did this."

"What?"

"LUCAS. YOU DREW ALL OVER MY CAST! I look like I just got back from a middle school church camp!"

I hold it up for both of us to inspect. He's taken a Sharpie and defaced the entire surface with hearts and quotes.

I love Lucas

Marry me, Lucas

Daisy+Lucas=<3

"Looks like the lovesick ramblings of a teenage girl to me. Are you sure you didn't do that in your sleep?"

"Ha ha," I say, having calmed down enough to appreciate the fact that I would have done the exact same thing to him. "Well played. It is objectively funny that your face now covers my forearm. You even did some shading. Kudos. Now give me the stupid Sharpie."

He points to the uncapped pen sitting on the counter. "All out of ink, I'm afraid."

Another useless card from his wallet gets tossed into the trash.

He is completely placid, but his straight face is betrayed

by a slight curl at the side of his mouth. He is pleased with my panicked attempts to resuscitate the Sharpie.

"Come on. Come on!" I slap it on the edge of the counter, trying to shake out any ink lodged at the bottom of the pen. I lick the felt tip and cringe at the taste.

"Huh, I guess it wasn't dead after all," he says, eyeing my new tongue tattoo.

After I wash the taste of ink from my mouth, I stay in the bathroom, deciding how to proceed. Blacking the entire thing out will be time-consuming and ugly.

Besides, I am more creative than that.

Every instance of *I heart Lucas* becomes *I heart George Lucas*.

The large portrait of his face is surprisingly easy to transform into an abstract interpretation of R2-D2.

The hearts he has scribbled along the sides become tiny Death Stars.

My graffitied cast is now an homage to Star Wars, and when I walk back into the exam room, Lucas acknowledges my craftiness with a nod.

"You seemed pretty eager to hide the fact that you heart me. Doth the lady protest too much?"

"The lady protests the exact right amount. Now if you'll excuse me, I'm going to hang out by the air vent, because I'm slightly high from all those fumes. Also, I think if I angle myself just right, I can pretend you don't exist."

HOUR 9

It's 9:00 PM, not exactly time for sleep, but I am eager to be done with the day. We've covered the small glass window on the exam room door with a drape to block out the light from the hallway.

"Hey! Whoa! Slow down there, stripasaurus rex," I bellow.

He turns over his shoulder. "Sorry. Can't sleep with jeans on."

"Oh *come on*."

"Why would I lie about that?"

I don't have time to answer because he's already unzipping his pants and sliding them down his legs. I turn away, but not before catching sight of his ass, clad in tight black boxer briefs. His shirt goes next and I'm met by an expanse of naked flesh. Broad shoulders. A smooth, tan back that tapers down near his waist. I look away. Then chance another quick peek. I shouldn't have. Suddenly, I think they've cut off the air supply to our room. I suck in a deep breath then release it slowly, so he doesn't notice.

I turn to face the ceiling and pull my CDC-issued blanket a little higher. In truth, I don't want to sleep in my jean shorts either. As soon as Lucas closes his eyes, I'll hop off the exam table and slip them off surreptitiously.

When I hear Lucas situate himself on the cot, I turn just enough that I can see his naked chest and shoulders over the top of the bristly army green blanket. From my perch on the exam table, I have a perfect view of him. Growing up, I saw his bare chest a hundred times at cross country practices, swimming parties. It never bothered me before, but this version of Lucas where he could be a stunt double for Henry Cavill really makes it hard to focus elsewhere. I *really* want to touch him, to run my hand across his tan skin.

I brush the thought away and silence another deep breath.

I won't be able to sleep. I sit up and decide that if I

change, I'll feel better. I take a blue medical gown into the bathroom and when I walk back out, Lucas is staring at the ceiling with his hands behind his head. I stand at the end of his cot and slowly, his gaze drops to me. He smiles as he sees my makeshift pajamas.

"Cute."

I inch closer to his cot and finger the scratchy material of my gown. He sits up and the blanket falls to his waist. In the dim light he looks like a wicked dream. Sharp jaw. Ruffled brown hair. Toned chest. The air sizzles and we're not in an exam room anymore. We're in a dream, one where I'm not at war with Lucas Thatcher.

No.

No. No. No.

I shake away every intrusive thought springing to mind. *Step closer. Bend low and straddle him on that cot—*

"Daisy…"

Lucas says my name and my eyes flick up to his. My thoughts are written across my cheeks. They burn with a blush I'm helpless to contain. His eyes narrow like he's trying to read me. Of course he can. To him, I'm an open book.

I want you so bad, my body says.

I shake my head and try to move past the cot, but then Lucas' hand catches mine. His fingers tighten around my wrist. He doesn't say a word, but he doesn't have to. The second his skin touches mine, I'm his.

And then I'm having an out-of-body experience, because my head is telling me to keep walking, to climb onto the exam table, and go to sleep…and yet, my body is doing something different. My intrusive thoughts have finally become intrusive actions.

I'm not sure who moves first. His hand is there,

wrapping around my forearm and tugging me down, but I am already on my way.

My knees fall on either side of his hips so I straddle him, just like I so desperately wanted them to. Together, we barely fit, but he keeps ahold of my hips and I know he's got me.

For so long, I don't move. Petrified. He squeezes my hips and tries to meet my eyes, but I'm staring at his chest. My non-casted hand reaches out and drags across the bare skin. It's hard, a wall of muscle, but I can feel his heart beating a wild rhythm beneath my palm. I linger there, amazed by the effect I have on him, but he's growing impatient. His hands twist circles on my lower back, working the material of my gown into a jumbled mess near my hips.

I retaliate by brushing his blanket lower, exposing his abs. He is a truly superhuman. Divine. My hands are there, brushing across every inch of him. Soon I will come to my senses and leap off the cot, but for now, I'm suspended in a dream.

He's done with the patient game though. His hand trails up my spine and he nudges me forward until my chest falls to his. We fit perfectly and I'm so glad I took my bra off when I changed into the gown. We're naked, separated by a thin gown, and the sensation is so sensual that warmth blooms low between my legs. I brush my chest against his with my eyes closed, greedy for more. I am behind enemy lines and I feel alive. Just how turned on can he make me? I want to find out.

My breasts are heavy, full, and then his hands are there, sliding from my back to cup one and then the other from the outside of my gown. I can feel the warmth of his palms radiate through the material. His hands are so big.

Confident. He rolls over my nipples and I arch against him like a greedy cat. He's patient, *practiced*. Better than I imagined he could be.

The fact that we're silent doesn't shock me. We're walking a tightrope. We're holding our breaths. Our weaponized words will only upset the delicate peace we've built.

I won't tell if you won't, I signal with a roll of my hips.

His groan is a legal contract, signed at the dotted line.

My gown is like a bikini, and by undoing two simple ties behind my neck and behind my back, I could be naked from the waist up.

He goes for the loose knot around my back first. With a flick of his wrist, the bow is gone, and the present is nearly unwrapped. He revels in the anticipation, gliding his hands across my naked back, up around my ribs, and then he's cupping my breasts from behind the drape of fabric. He brushes the center of his palm across my nipple, back and forth, gently teasing. It's an erotic little game, the way he leaves the tie around my neck. He gets to feel, but not see. Touch, but not taste.

I sit back and press my hand to his chest. He's hard muscle beneath warm, golden skin—and all this time, I thought he was cold-blooded. His eyes meet mine and they are a shade of brown I've never seen. I shiver and he grows harder beneath me.

How far will you go? I ask with an arch of my brow. *How much can you take?*

His hands drift up to my neck and he yanks the last tie free. *Yes*, I think, *diving into the lion's den*. God yes. I want Lucas to see me. Everything. Loose material gathers around my waist and whatever peace there was is gone. There is danger in his eyes, not from malice but from hunger. He takes me in, from flushed cheeks to quivering stomach. It's all there for him to see. Every invisible scar from our war.

"Daisy," he whispers, hoarse.

Suddenly, I feel like a toy that's been wound and wound and wound.

I'm ready to be set free.

I *need* to be.

I reach down, take his hand from around my waist, and slide it right over the middle of my belly. With my guidance, it slips down inside the loose gown, just over the damp material of my panties. My thighs are spread over his and silk separates his fingers from me. My eyes squeeze close. My mouth drops open. There's a low gasp, and it's me, shocked by how good it feels to have his thumb circle there. Gently at first, just a hint of what's to come. Soft circles that tease, around and around the exact spot where I need him to be. He's getting closer and with a smirk, I realize Lucas somehow knows exactly how to touch me. *Know thy enemy* takes on new meaning for me. I tilt my head back and the pressure builds, the steam rises, and in my mind I'm reaching for the release valve. I stretch, I'm almost there, I…

A sharp, loud knock on the door is a pinprick to our balloon.

I shriek and leap off him, stumbling. I yank my gown back to cover my chest, only then remembering we covered the window to block the hallway light. We're hidden.

"Hey! Are you two okay in there?" the CDC official asks. Apparently *now* he has time for questions. "Did you get the cot set up?"

"For fuck's sake," Lucas hisses under his breath, sitting up and yanking his hands through his hair.

Another knock indicates that we're supposed to answer.

"Fine!" Lucas shouts. "Sleeping!"

"Oh, sorry about that. Night."

My sympathetic nervous system, reacting to a cocktail of stress and excitement, has flooded my bloodstream with adrenaline. As a result, my heart rate and blood pressure are through the roof, my pupils are saucers, my lungs have expanded. It's my body's way of asking *fight or flight*, but from the way things were headed with Lucas, I know I was gearing up for a different f-word entirely.

I begin to normalize, but remember I have nowhere to go. I'm in a 10x12 cage, with Lucas, who is currently looking at me, waiting for me to speak.

"Daisy? Should we—"

I turn before he can finish and scurry back into the bathroom to retie my gown. Then I think better of it and put another one on over it, backward. I'm a teenager, doubling up on protection because I think it will safeguard me. It won't.

When I walk back into the room, Lucas is on his side, facing away from me.

Apparently, there's nothing left to say. With *fuck* gone and *flight* off the table, there is only one option left for us to turn to.

I climb onto the exam table, trying to be as quiet as possible, like maybe I can trick Lucas into thinking I'm not in the room anymore. I really don't want to talk about what just happened, but the air didn't get that memo.

The room is electrified and every movement Lucas makes sparks through me.

I don't fall asleep. I lie there on tenterhooks, waiting for him to speak, yell—anything. We've never been closer, but in this moment I feel a gulf between us larger than the 11 years we spent apart.

HOUR 18

In the morning, Lucas is in a sour mood, probably upset that he had to go to sleep with a hard-on. BFD. We all thought the night would end better than it did.

"Can you pass the eggs?" I ask genially.

He tosses the pack of powdered eggs my way without a word.

"Cheers," I grumble.

I don't comment on his adorable bedhead or the fact that he hasn't put his t-shirt back on. At least his jeans are covering half of him. I fork dehydrated eggs into my mouth and tell myself they don't taste like kitty litter.

Through the morning, we avoid each other as much as our cell allows. I fashion a friend for Gary named Glenda. I prop the stuffed exam gloves up on the counter, and it looks as if they're holding little thumb hands. *Great*, I think, *even inanimate objects are less dysfunctional than me and Lucas.*

HOUR 22

Gary and Glenda are in the trash and Lucas has cabin fever. He's pacing the room while rolling his shoulders and exuding clear *leave me the hell alone* pheromones. I want to ask him if he's okay, but I think he'll jump on me if I do and I'm not ready for a repeat of last night. I feel queasy just thinking about it.

Whatever.

His mental health isn't my concern. Besides, in a few

hours, we're free.

"Wee-ooh, wee-ooh," I intone like a warning siren after he accidentally kicks a dozen tongue depressors out of line. I pretend my fingers are missiles, launching in retaliation for the border violation. My index fingers loop and spin to the crude sounds of rocket thrust before taking aim at his nose. They halt an inch before contact, frozen by the glare he's leveled at me.

His brows are pinched together, forming an angry line down the middle of his forehead. I cower.

"All's forgiven," I say with a shrug and a half-smile. "I'll just straighten those out again."

Note to self: Lucas is not in the mood for games. Just ask Gary and Glenda.

HOUR 23

I don't like this new, angry version of Lucas. He's hotheaded and rude. He hasn't spoken a single word to me in hours and it's starting to get to me. As I change back into my jean shorts and t-shirt in the bathroom, I consider how far I'm willing to go to get the old Lucas back. It involves swallowing my pride.

He's dressed in his jeans and a t-shirt when I walk back out, but his face is no more relaxed. He's standing beside the exam table flipping through a *Highlights*.

I wait for him to look up and acknowledge me, but to him, I'm invisible.

"Yes," I say.

He flips another page.

When I say what I'm about to say, I need him to look at me.

I walk over to him and don't stop until I'm nearly on top of him. No chance of him ignoring me now.

"Lucas."

He looks up—barely, but I take it anyway.

"Truth: yes, I fantasize about our kiss in the hallway."

He arches a brow, studies me for all of three seconds, and then looks back down at his magazine. It's like I've said nothing at all.

"Didn't you just hear me? I fantasize about the kiss. I want you to kiss me again! Stop—just stop pretending to spot the differences! They've already been found!"

I yank the magazine out of his hand and fling it across the exam room. It lands with a *plop* on the tile.

I think I've finally got his attention. He crosses his arms and stares at me. Silent.

I want to scream.

"I fantasize about our kiss! How crazy is that?"

He shakes his head and leans forward, bringing his lips dangerously close to mine. "I heard you the first time."

And then he pulls away and stands back up.

Just like that.

Like I didn't just ask him to kiss me.

Who the hell does he think he is?

I crowd him in against the exam table and fist his t-shirt in my palm. I try to tug his face down to me again, and for two seconds, he doesn't budge. Then he humors me and leans down. We're face to face. Almost mouth to mouth. My eyes scorch into his. He seems amused.

"You listen here, Lucas Thatcher. I hate you, but you're going to kiss me. You're going to kiss me and you're not going to stop."

He smiles and then I think he's going to laugh, but I don't let him. I press onto my tiptoes and crash my mouth against his. It's punishment. Tough love. I am kissing him for his own good.

He's frozen at first, confused. I am kissing a mouth that is not kissing back and I die of embarrassment just before his hands lock onto my hips and he tugs me closer. I stumble into him and paste myself against his hard body. *Oh thank god*, I think just as his head tilts and his teeth find my bottom lip. He's been bad, but I'm willing to share the punishment.

He bites and I squeeze my thighs together.

Be good, I warn my body. We will kiss, but nothing more.

When his hands start to tug my shirt up across my stomach and ribs, I justify it because cotton is truly a difficult fiber to kiss in. My jean shorts? Those are in the way too.

We are the type of unpredictable frenzy that scares me. My fingers tingle, my toes curl. My heart is in my throat and my stomach flips alongside it. I string my fingers through his thick hair and he growls into my mouth. It's the sexiest sound I've ever heard and it earns him one leg, then two wrapped around his waist. That's right, Lucas—with good behavior like that, I might just commute your sentence.

Finding myself coiled around Lucas Thatcher like a python would normally shock me, but at the moment there are other emotions fighting for my attention. Fear and anxiety both try to wrestle for first place, but lust wins.

My panties brush against his jeans and the sensation is one I will never forget. It's rough and merciless. Solid. He's as hard as he was last night and I will not let anyone interrupt us this time. I am all too aware the officials might knock and let us out any second, so I yank his shirt up over his head and make my intentions clear: keep going or die.

He turns and presses me up against the exam room wall. There's no apology as the textured paint scratches my back and his stubble turns the skin on my neck crimson.

His lips feel familiar, even against a place on my body they've never been. They attend to my chin and then my neck, lower and lower until he kisses my breasts through my thin bra. *It's still technically a kiss*, I tell myself, proud of my logic. His tongue wets the lace and it turns translucent. My tight nipples are completely visible and I'm so obviously sensitive there. He exploits the knowledge, sucking and licking with ease, so confident with his mouth that I'm convinced he's taken lessons at some point.

With his mouth occupied, his strong hands have taken charge of exploration. He alternates between light caresses and forceful pressure, as if to remind me that he's still dangerous. He leans back and I watch him slowly drag his gaze across my chest and then lower, between my legs. My panties aren't much, but they're the last barrier I have. He reaches down and brushes his knuckle across my center. My mouth drops open. Closes. My teeth sink into my lip so I don't scream something inappropriate. If I thought his jeans felt good, it doesn't compare to his touch, his finger brushing the material aside, pausing for an eternity at my wetness, and then sinking into me.

"I've always wanted you wrapped around my finger."

My mouth drops open again but no sound escapes.

Lucas Thatcher has never owned me as much as he does in this moment.

He has won, and from his smirk, he knows it—but he's not greedy. He's going to share the prize. He's going to make me feel as good as he does. His long middle finger slides in deep and then drags slowly back out. This is how it's always been with Lucas—who can go the deepest, who can get there the fastest? My non-casted hand grips his shoulder. His neck. His bicep. I try to stabilize myself with anything I can, but he's going too fast, drawing out pleasurable tingles that I can't hide.

His head falls to the crook of my neck and his breath warms my ear. His finger circles and circles, dipping inside me and bringing the slickness back up to my most sensitive spot. Another few circles and I will come undone for him.

"You're close," he rasps, more command than statement.

I wish I could correct him, but it's true.

My teeth sink into his shoulder as the first sparks start to fly. He's telling me to come and I am coming and his fingers keep up their pace and I'm shaking in his arms, trying to grip on to every ripple. He circles and circles until the very last burst of pleasure has washed over me, and then I'm limp in his arms and he's kissing my neck, just below my ear. His lips are tender and sweet. He's not gloating like I assumed he would.

Which means he deserves a little reward of his own.

I let my legs fall from around his waist. I can barely put any weight on them, not after what he's just done to me, so I sink down to my knees.

Some women say giving oral is an act of submission or subservience to men. As Lucas' eyes widen in shock and his mouth drops open, I realize I've never disagreed more. There, on my knees, I hold all the power I can possibly carry, and more.

He asks what I'm doing—as if any guy is confused when a woman looks up from beneath her eyelashes, tugging at the buckle of his jeans. He asks more as a courtesy. In this instance, *What are you doing?* means *Are you sure?*

I refuse to answer him. I unbuckle his jeans and tug them down along with his boxer briefs. I'm not as patient as he was. After all, there's no time to tease when the CDC could come in at any moment.

Lucas Thatcher is hard in my hand. So very large. I smirk up at him; no wonder he's an overconfident ass. He doesn't see me looking up at him though. His head has fallen back against the wall. His eyes are closed. His brows are pinched and his lips have fallen open on an exhale. He is a Baroque sculpture: *The Ecstasy of Lucas Thatcher*.

I glide my closed palm over him, up and down until he grows another inch in my hand. It's the sort of thing I always wanted—Lucas under my control—I just never thought it would happen like this.

I wrap my lips around the tip of him and then I take him deeper into my mouth. The first taste is almost enough to break us both.

"*God, Daisy.*"

He isn't sure who to worship, but I'll have him convinced soon enough. I wrap my palm around the base of his shaft and slide my mouth on and off him. I move slowly, dragging out every movement just like he did with me. It's sensual, having him in my mouth like that. I taste him on my tongue and I close my eyes, trying to seduce him as best as possible.

His fingers string through my hair, tightening when I hit just the right spot.

You like that, don't you.

I toy with him; I can't help it.

Then his hand reaches down and cups the back of my head. He's finished with games.

I smirk and take him deeper, pumping him with my

hand.

He doesn't ease up and my breaths are starting to get labored. I grip the back of his thighs and let him fuck my mouth. It's an intimate act, trusting him not to hurt me.

"This is what I've wanted," he says, caressing my cheek.

I close my eyes so he can't read the emotion in them.

And then he's coming. No lead-in. No warning.

I barely register anything but the sound coming from his mouth. The deep, satisfied groan. The way his hips buck forward, slipping out of his control. He is completely lost in me and I make sure it stays that way. For so long, we hover there, regaining our breath. I stay on my knees, staring up at him, and he finally looks down at me. It's the first time we've locked eyes since I kissed him and the intimacy of the eye contact is more shocking than anything we've done yet. The delayed vulnerability finds its target, and self-preservation takes over.

I look away and stand.

I lock myself in the bathroom, staring at my reflection in the mirror. I am red and raw. My breath is still labored, recovering. My lips are a little swollen, carrying the evidence of what I've done, and my eyes are dilated. I'm still in shock.

I lean forward and splash water across my face. It feels good so I do it a few more times. I'm drying my hands when Lucas knocks on the door and informs me that they're ready to confirm our negative skin tests, and then we'll be free to go. How's that for timing?

I imagine a parade waiting for us outside, a bevy of local and national reporters fighting over each other to get the scoop. America will be so glad to see us free and safe that they'll declare today a national holiday. Yet when we stroll out of the clinic—not making eye contact, keeping our distance—the sidewalk is empty, and the only parade is the procession of new emotional baggage we each drag behind us. So much for my fifteen minutes of fame.

To her credit, my mom is across the street at Hamilton Brew. When she sees me, she waves a plastic bag overhead.

"Daisy! I brought you clean underwear!"

The universe can be so cruel at times.

R︮x

CHAPTER EIGHTEEN

LUCAS

From: lucasthatcher@stanford.edu
To: daisybell@duke.edu
Subject: #351

Sometimes lying to yourself can be helpful. Therapeutic, even. But there are some moments in life when the truth is so white-hot that you don't even have the choice to ignore it. It demands to be heard.

So ask yourself, Daisy: do you regret what happened?
I don't.

For a few hours, you finally stopped fighting an imaginary war inside that beautiful mind of yours. You let go of all the things that *shouldn't be* and guess what? It was sexy as hell. I wouldn't be surprised if you've already convinced yourself it was some kind of defeat. But don't worry, Daisy. Even though you were on your knees in that exam room, I was the one trembling. I had your blonde hair wrapped up in my hands. Your delicate features were so serene, so focused on what you were doing. Your heart-shaped mouth. Your lips...

Jesus, Daisy.

It's no wonder you freaked out afterward. Those big blue eyes caught mine and you froze. I don't think we've ever been closer than in that moment.

So I'm not going to stop now.

Not when I know how good it can be. How true. You'll see.

℞

CHAPTER NINETEEN

As a courtesy, Dr. McCormick gives Lucas and me the day off on Monday so we can recover from the quarantine. Apparently, Mr. Holder is doing well down in Houston and I'm glad, but I can't seem to think of anything beyond what happened in that exam room. It's eating away at me.

My mom gets suspicious because I don't get excited about homemade chicken pot pie on Monday night. In fact, I barely eat any of it. I sit across from her at our dining table as she regales me with stories of her weekend without me and I only seem to catch every other word, like she's talking through a bad cell connection. She knows something is off, and I think that's why she calls Madeleine over. She's the special forces unit.

She arrives when I'm back upstairs, standing at my bedroom window and staring at Lucas' childhood room next door. With his curtains drawn, I can't see much.

"We can do this the easy way or the hard way," Madeleine declares, walking into my room with a bag in her hands.

From inside, she extracts a bottle of wine, chocolate, and sour gummy worms.

I don't pick up on her ploy until I've made my choice

and ripped open the bag of worms.

"Oh god. Something's really wrong," she says, shaky hand covering her mouth like I've just announced a terminal cancer diagnosis.

I toss the bag back on my bed and reach for the chocolate instead.

"It's too late! You grabbed the worms! What the hell is going on?"

You see, Madeleine knows my tells: wine is for every day; chocolate is for your average, run-of-the-mill bad day; but gummy worms—those are for red alert, code black situations.

I don't see a point in tiptoeing around the truth. My thoughts have been circling themselves all day. Her opinion might help.

"Lucas and I nearly had sex when we were in quarantine."

After my sentence settles in my room, I think she has a mini stroke because her left eye starts to twitch and her mouth goes slack. I hold out a finger and tell her to follow my movements, but she shoves it away and grips my shoulders.

"What did you just say?" she asks, trying to shake sense into me.

"Lucas and I fooled around. Ow. Okay. Back off. Twice, actually. I think we would have had sex too if the CDC hadn't been so punctual."

"Ew!" She finally steps away and shakes away the images swirling around her head. Her hands cover her ears. "No. No. No. I don't want to think about my brother doing that."

"And you think I do?! We were practically forced into it!"

"What do you mean you were *forced*? Was that part of the CDC infection protocol? Boning your arch nemesis?"

"There was no way around it. What little air we had in there was thick enough to cut with a scalpel. The two of us just aren't meant to be locked in like that—it could have just as easily ended with murder."

"Are you being serious right now?"

"Yes. With that in mind, I suppose we should consider ourselves lucky. Honestly, Madeleine, it ruined every assumption I had about why he hasn't been able to hold down a girlfriend all these years. The guy has skills."

"STOP."

"Sorry, you're my only friend. You have to listen."

"No. It's not healthy."

"Oh please. You were the one who wanted me to make nice with him! Well guess what, we made nice all right. We made nice all over that freaking exam room!"

Madeleine has fallen onto my bed and burrowed beneath my pillows to try to block out the sound of my voice. I continue anyway.

"I've been thinking about it a lot since they released us and I've decided it doesn't change anything. I still hate him."

"Of course."

"Truthfully, the fact that he is skilled in that department pisses me off even more."

"So what are you going to do when you see him at work tomorrow?"

"What do you think I'm going to do, Madeleine? Behave like the adult that I am. Since nothing has changed, I won't change the way I conduct myself. Nothing has changed. One more time, say it with me: *nothing has changed.*"

"You don't sound very confident."

"Well by tomorrow morning, I will. Now pass me those gummy worms."

When I stroll into Dr. McCormick's office the next day, I am the picture of professionalism. I'm wearing my smartest black fitted pants and a cream silk blouse. My heels give me a few inches and my white coat has been freshly starched. I have brushed up on all the patients we will be seeing and I've confirmed there is ink in every one of my pens.

Lucas has done the same. His hair is somehow thicker than usual. More brown. Begging for my hands. His jaw is freshly shaved, and his glasses rest confidently on the bridge of his nose. He's a Ken doll masquerading as a doctor and it bothers me that he probably wakes up like this.

"You're avoiding me," he says as I brush past him in the kitchen. My mug is steaming with freshly poured coffee.

I pat his shoulder. "Not any more than usual, Dr. Thatcher. You're highly avoidable."

He reaches out and catches my hand before I can scurry back to my office. "I like that top you have on. How far do you think the buttons will fly when I rip if off?"

"Yes," I reply, raising my voice. "I *did* have a good weekend. Thank you for asking."

Dr. McCormick turns into the kitchen. I heard him coming down the hall before Lucas did. I smirk and he steps back, releasing my hand.

Dr. McCormick smiles cheerfully as he refills his coffee cup. He is jollier by the day, probably excited about the prospect of impending retirement. "Good to see you two getting along this morning. Quarantine must have done you some good."

"I think Dr. Bell enjoyed it more than I did," Lucas replies. "At least, she was more vocal about it."

His double entendre rushes past with all the subtlety of a freight train, but Dr. McCormick offers no sign of recognition. I dig the heel of my shoe into his foot before turning away.

"Dr. Thatcher was the real trooper. In fact, confinement seemed to suit him. I think he would do well in prison."

Dr. McCormick laughs. "I guess some things never change."

Fifteen minutes later, Lucas and I are standing in the hallway, prepping to go see our first patient. It's 7:55 AM and I am hot. Bothered. My picture of professionalism is devolving into more of a porny polaroid.

"Would you stop?" I blurt out, angry.

"Stop what?" he asks.

Practiced innocence drips from his chiseled features.

"Stop looking at me like you've seen me naked," I hiss under my breath.

His mouth perks up. "I don't think Pandora's box works like that. How would you prefer me to look at you?"

"Like before. With hatred. A dash of contempt."

"How about this?"

"Worse."

With him standing right beside me, his chest pressed against my arm, I'm swaying like a haphazard stack of blocks. A clumsy toddler could knock me on my ass.

"Just look the other way will you? I'm trying to finish

reading this chart."

"I've already gone over it. Mr. Nichols. 58. Routine annual exam. Can I look at you again?"

"He didn't mention any complaints on the intake form? And no. Nothing changes between us. What happened in that exam room stays in that exam room."

"No complaints. He's fit as a fiddle. I agree, the exam room is off-limits, so how about you meet me in my office at lunch instead? I'd like a round two, and from the way you've been eyeing me all morning, I know you would too."

My eyes widen at his brazenness. It is said that eyes are the windows to the soul, but in that moment they expose my libido. I wish I had curtains.

I knock on Mr. Nichols' door and stride in. It's Lucas' turn to take the lead.

"Good morning, Mr. Nichols. I'm Dr. Thatcher and this is my associate, Dr. Bell."

"Why's there two of you?"

I hold up my casted hand, which is now a blacked-out mess thanks to my attempt to cover up Lucas' handiwork. The Star Wars cover-up was only temporary; I needed his handwriting and his hearts off my sleeve.

I perch in the corner while Lucas starts the annual. He's listening to Mr. Nichols' heart when I realize with a start that we're back at the scene of the crime. This is *the* exam room. Mariah has replaced the *Highlights* magazines with fresh editions and my tongue depressor line is long gone. The rest is just as we left it. The wall where Lucas had me pinned is right in front of me. Taunting. When I blink, I see us there: Lucas pressed up against me, grinding his hips against mine. I see my head thrown back against the wall and his hands stripping me bare. I'm naked and his mouth is on me. Hot and wet. Dipping lower, making me moan.

The pop of a nitrile glove snaps me back to reality.

Lucas is done with the annual. He's assuring Mr. Nichols that we'll use an in-network lab for his workup. He's leading me out of the exam room after him and I'm only a touch more cognizant than a houseplant.

"You look pale," Lucas says.

There is concern in his voice—*concern*!

So I grip the lapel of his white coat and drag him after me. The hallway is empty and his office is too. It's tinier than mine. I've never been inside because I never had a reason to go in before, but now I have a reason and that reason is inconveniently located between my legs.

I confirm no one spotted us slip inside and then I close the door tight. Click. We are alone. I lock it too. We are *really* alone. Lucas is shocked.

But I'm already stripping off my white coat.

"Listen Romeo, I'm only using you," I say.

My white coat is tossed onto his chair.

"I want to get inside your head, dull your edge," I continue.

My silk blouse is inverted over my head and tossed to the floor.

"I need you to fall for me. I want you to hand your heart over willingly so I can break it. That way, you'll leave and give me the practice."

My pants are unbuttoned and I'm stepping out of them.

"It's the oldest trick in the book, Lucas."

I stand before him in a matching lace set that I put on that morning for no good reason. His gaze devours me from across the small space. His hands fist. Relax. Fist again. Then his mouth curls and he starts to strip off his white coat.

"What a coincidence, Daisy. *I'm* only using *you*," he declares.

He tosses his coat onto the back of his chair and my stomach dips.

"I want to fuck with you. Make you fall in love with me."

He steps toward me.

"So that when I break *your* heart, you'll leave and give *me* the practice."

My heart is pounding in my ears. My knees are shaking. His hands cup my neck and he tilts my head back so that his next few words are delivered right against my mouth.

"And believe me, I *really* want to fuck with you."

My knees give out at the exact moment Lucas turns me around and hauls me against him. I'm a toy in his arms. Pliable. Bendable. His hands wrap around my chest and caress my breasts through my bra. He's rough. Possessive. I reach up and string my hand through his hair as he tugs the cups down and takes my bare breasts in his hands. They're heavy in his palms, filling up his grip, and he groans in satisfaction, so very pleased.

He kisses my shoulder and circles his palms, tightening on my nipples so that when he drags his hands lower, the evidence of his touch lingers behind.

If he appreciates the size of my breasts, I appreciate the size of his hands. They grip my waist like I'm nothing. They press me in, caging me between him and his desk. His left hand reaches back up for my breast and his right hand flattens against my navel. He dips lower. Steady. Gentle.

My lace panties are thin, nothing against him. His hand slips around and covers my warmth over the lace. My belly clenches. My nerve endings sizzle.

I'm not aware of any sound escaping from my lips until

his left hand leaves my breast and covers my mouth.

"You'll get us caught," he warns. "Then nobody wins."

The warning should scare me, but I left reality the moment I stepped inside his office. Maybe he knows it because he doesn't remove his left hand as his right one glides back and forth between my legs. The heel of his palm passes over my center, right over my bundle of nerves, and I buck against him. He whispers in my ear.

"Should I try that again?"

I'm nodding like a fool.

He smiles against my neck and drags his hand back and forth, back and forth. Each region of his palm provides a different texture. Hard. Soft. Abrasive. Smooth.

I think he's going to make me come like this until his hand hooks inside my panties and he tugs them to one side of my inner thigh. One finger becomes two and he's fucking me like that, against his desk.

I try to fall forward, to rest my upper body on the cold wood, but he keeps me pressed against him. I shiver when he slips two fingers in, and again as he slowly drags them out. My desire seeps from a place of primal instinct, of intuition. My neolithic brain is reduced to basic impulses. Moaning. Gasping. Clenching.

"I'm going to make you come like this, Daisy. Just like this."

Sounds like a fucking plan, I want to shout at him.

But then his fingers pump faster and my retort sounds a lot like, *Yes. Please. God, Lucas.*

A ripple of desire travels from the base of my neck to the very tip of my spine and he feels it. He uses it as an excuse to go harder, faster. I'm sweaty against his chest. My fingers are tugging strands of his hair hard enough to yank them free. I'm close and I need him to know it. I'm feeling those first few tendrils of pleasure, such an intoxicating promise of what's to come in a few seconds. If only he keeps going. If only he touches the exact right spot. If only his left hand slips up to circle my nipple and the added sensation is a catapult.

I.

Am.

There.

His mouth captures my earlobe and he gently bites as I grind my hips against the palm of his hand. Again and again, I shake and shudder against him. One wave carries into another and eventually my soft cries turn to panting, and then my breathing starts to steady.

"We have another patient," he reminds me, amused.

My eyes pop open and I'm back at work. Dr. McCormick is right on the other side of the door, talking to Mariah in the kitchen. I step out of his reach, hit the desk, step back into him, and then sort of volley around like a short-circuiting robot. I've yet to regain my motor skills.

"Right, the patient."

I feign calmness as I run in small circles, gathering my clothes. My blouse is so wrinkled that a few shakes won't cut it. I tuck it back into my pants and then try to conceal as much of it as possible under my white coat. I don't even dare think of what my hair and makeup must look like now. And Lucas? My eyes avoid him by any means possible.

"I'm glad we're on the same page," Lucas says, reaching out to straighten my white coat and then tucking a few strands of my long hair behind my ear.

"Yes." My voice is shaky. "My thoughts exactly."

As we slip stealthily back out into the hallway, I realize I have no clue what page that is, or even which book I could find it in.

The 7 Habits of Highly Dysfunctional Enemies?
Chicken Soup for the Horny Soul?

℞
CHAPTER TWENTY

At lunch the next day, Lucas comes into my office uninvited and drops a steaming mug of coffee on my desk. He's even taken the time to add a splash of cream.

"What is that?" I ask, keeping my attention on the mug and not Lucas standing beside my chair.

"Coffee."

A small kindness from him feels like a diamond ring.

I push the thought aside and reach for the plate of coffee cake I saved for him.

"Cake," I say, handing the plate over to him.

I'm amused by the fact that we're feeding and caffeinating each other like an old couple. Considering the events of the last few days, I suspect we're subconsciously keeping our energy up in anticipation of impromptu office orgasms.

I take a sip of my coffee and he takes a bite of cake. We hold eye contact while we do it, like we know it's poisoned.

The coffee is just the right temperature.

"Do you own jeans?" I ask casually, motioning to his pressed slacks.

"I had them on during quarantine."

On second thought, the coffee is too hot. I set it down with a sigh.

"Well put some on Saturday evening. You and Madeleine are coming to game night. My mom has been insisting."

It's a lie—she hasn't brought it up in weeks. It's my idea. It's too late to ignore Lucas, and for the time being, it's impossible to put any space between us. So, I've decided to use controlled environments to study him, to see if I can figure out his motive for acting the way he has. It's the closest thing to a date that enemies can have.

"What if I'm busy on Saturday?" he asks coyly.

"That would make me the happiest girl in the world," I say, clasping my hands in mock prayer.

"I'll let you know."

He's posturing, but I already know his answer. Criminals can't help but want to return to the scene of the crime.

"You do that," I say, turning so he can't see my smile.

My mom is tickled pink that I am not only willing to attend game night, but that I'm taking the initiative to plan it.

On Friday night, we're at the grocery store getting supplies. "We need appetizers and finger foods. Lots of drinks. Definitely Jack and Coke."

"Isn't that Lucas' favorite drink?" my mom asks.

"Everyone likes that drink, Mom."

"Not me, gives me acid reflux."

"Okay, everyone under fifty likes it."

By the time we leave, our cart is overloaded with party

supplies. I look like a contestant on *Supermarket Sweep*, and the cashier asks if we're having a big party.

"A rager," I lie.

The next morning, Lucas is mowing my mother's lawn again and I am standing at the window with a cup of coffee, watching. Our neighbor across the street, Mrs. Betty is doing the same. I tip my mug to her and she smiles. It's a silent agreement: *I won't tell if you won't.*

"Enjoying the view?" my mom asks, coming up behind me.

At first, I panic, afraid I've been caught—but then I remember I'm not doing anything wrong.

"Just making sure he doesn't mess up."

"Well c'mon. I need your help."

She puts me to work. For the entire day, I clean and cook. I whip up chicken salad and guacamole. I spruce the pillows on the couch, step back, and then spruce them again. I meticulously hide any childhood photo that portrays me in a bad light, and I help in the kitchen in between it all.

Madeleine is the real champion. She shows up around lunchtime with champagne and orange juice for mimosas and I greedily accept her offering. I sip glass after glass until I've got a perfect buzz going. The pressure of planning game night is now a dull memory.

"Why is this such a big deal for you?" Madeleine asks when we go upstairs to get changed.

"It's not."

"You cut each sandwich into a heart."

"I thought they looked cute that way."

"You put balloons on the mailbox."

"It's a party, Madeleine. It's got to look festive!"

"You rearranged the furniture in the living room four times."

"Yes. My mom really needs to bring in a feng shui consultant. There's some pretty bad juju in this house."

"Uh huh. Here, turn and I'll zip you."

I don't tell Madeleine that I put an equal amount of thought into picking out the perfect dress. It's red, a color I usually avoid. I saw it hanging on a mannequin in a shop window downtown and I knew I had to have it. It's short and flirty and I've never worn anything like it.

"Daaamn Daisy," Madeleine says, stepping back to assess me.

I've only managed half a smile when something out on the front path catches my eye. Party guests!

I run to the window and peer down. With my mom and Madeleine already here, that only leaves Lucas and his parents...but the person walking up the path is an unexpected guest, someone my mother definitely didn't run past me.

"Kelly O'Connor?" Madeleine asks behind me, clearly in shock.

I try to set my hand on the window sill, miss, and hit my forehead on the window. Kelly looks up, startled, and I jump away from the window.

"What the hell is she doing here?!"

Kelly O'Connor. KELLY. O'CONNOR. First grade teacher. Chairman of the Hamilton Pumpkin Patch Festival. Beautiful. Sparkly. Has no enemies.

I need to have a word with my mother.

Fortunately, she's in the kitchen pouring chips into a

bowl. I corner her against the counter.

"Kelly O'Connor? Seriously?!"

She spins around, beaming. "Oh perfect, has she arrived?"

The bell rings, and I hear Madeleine go to greet her.

"What were you thinking inviting her? I *can't stand* Kelly."

"Oh c'mon, Kelly isn't so bad."

"She insisted on playing the baby Jesus in the church nativity play until she was *thirteen*. Even worse, everyone was happy to give her the part because she was so angelic. Am I seriously the only one in town that thought braces on *the Lamb of God* was a bit of a stretch?"

My mom laughs. "Well I thought she did a fine job as Jesus, and anyway, I didn't invite her for you."

It dawns on me like a slap in the face: my mom invited Kelly for Lucas.

If she hadn't birthed me, I would have murdered her right then.

I can't breathe. My dress was flirty, but now it's just constricting. I want to tear it off and expand my lungs to max capacity.

"Uninvite her," I demand. "Tell her there's been a death in the family."

In fact, there might be.

"She's in our living room, Daisy."

I squeeze my eyes closed and try to think. Kelly is as dumb as a doorknob. Maybe I could tell her the first game is hide-and-seek and convince her to hide in a bush for six hours. *You're the best at this game, Kelly. That's right, just curl right up, like you're in a manger half your size.*

"I'm confused. What exactly are you upset about?"

"You're trying to set him up with someone."

"And why does that upset *you*?"

"Because I want Lucas alone! Sad and miserable and defeated."

"Daisy…"

"Fine. Whatever. I just don't see him with Kelly. They're nothing alike."

"Oh? So who do you think I should have set him up with instead?"

"How about you try to, I don't know, set up your single daughter? It's not like I have guys banging down my door now that I'm home!"

A knock on our door comes a second later.

Knock-knock. Knuh-knock-knock. It's a chipper little song, which means it's not Lucas.

My mom is giddy. "That must be Patrick!"

Patrick? Who is Pat—

"*Patrick Brubacher?!*" I hiss as she slithers out of my weak hold. I'm so caught off guard that she slips right around me and into the living room. She completely ignores my question, but it doesn't matter. I hear Patrick's voice as soon as Madeleine lets him in.

Patrick is the male equivalent of Kelly O'Connor: weak, blond, blandly handsome, like a well-built shoe. He's a veterinarian who once rescued a dog from a well and nursed him back to health. You've seen the photo collages: day 1, the dog looks like a goner; day 30, he's wearing a spiffy red bandana and smiling alongside his new owner. Patrick is that owner.

"Daisy Bell? Goodness, is that you?"

Naturally, Patrick is delighted to see me. He's never felt an emotion other than delight.

I let him hug me and I smell his cologne. It's good. He's tall and his blond hair is cut short. His smile is his most prominent feature and I think that's fitting. Kelly stands behind him, waiting to get to me.

"Hi Kelly," I offer, immediately wishing I could try again with a bit more enthusiasm.

She doesn't notice though. How could she? She's programmed to carry out a binary existence: be pleasant, or be dead. And she's still breathing.

"I have to admit, it was a blast from the past when your mom invited me to a game night. It's been ages since I've seen you or Lucas."

My heart sinks. That means she agreed to come prior to seeing Lucas 2.0. The tall, hunky, man version will arrive any minute and I'm sure she'll be *pleasantly surprised*. With that realization, I hate my mother even more.

I step back from Kelly and Patrick as a firm knock sounds from the front door. Madeleine answers it and I stand frozen as Lucas strides into my house with his parents and Dr. McCormick in tow. I barely register the fact that my mom has invited our boss because Lucas is wearing jeans and a cobalt blue sweater. The cobalt blue is shocking, the color of Superman's suit. What the fuck, Lucas. What the fuck.

"Wow," Kelly whispers under her breath, blushing like a schoolgirl. She looks to me for support and then realizes I won't be joining her in lusting after Lucas. I'm his rival. "Oh, nevermind."

I let everyone finish introductions while I make myself a drink in the kitchen. I don't realize it's a Jack and Coke until Lucas comes up behind me and plucks it out of my hand.

"Since when do you like Jack Daniels?"

"Since when do you wear sweaters?"

Silence. My comeback is a little weak, but he gives it to

me.

"What are Kelly and Patrick doing here?"

"My mom invited them. For us."

"For what? Extra competition?"

"She thinks Kelly will woo you."

He laughs and my heart grows three sizes in my chest. With the added blood flow it provides, I work up the courage to look up at him. His brown hair is ridiculously adorable and wavy. His cheekbones seem sharper than ever. He brings my cup to his lips and takes a sip before handing it back to me. I want to throw it in his face but I also want to kiss him. Luckily I see Kelly eyeing us from the doorway to the kitchen and do neither. I know she wants to come over and chat with Lucas, wants to swoop in and bat her big brown eyes. The image of her smiling up at him churns my stomach.

"So that means Patrick is here for you?" he asks, bringing my attention back to him.

I toy with my cup. "Presumably. I think my mom is hoping he'll adopt me like a stray."

"You're too wild. You'd eat him alive."

I don't deny it.

My mom claps and announces the start of game night. As I walk back into the living room with Lucas trailing behind me, I realize she's rearranged things in the time it took Madeleine and me to get ready upstairs. So much for feng shui.

"Lucas, you'll sit there, and Daisy, you're here."

She's put us on opposite sides of the room and everyone laughs except for Lucas and me.

"You've hidden all the sharp objects, right?" Patrick laughs.

"Do you have a barrier we can put between them?" Mr.

Thatcher asks.

"Maybe a fence would be best," Kelly adds, looking around the room to confirm we find her funny. I want to tell her she killed it. The joke is over.

"All right, c'mon," Lucas says with an easy smile. "We've both agreed to keep things civil, right Daisy?"

That's what he says, but my brain twists his words into foreplay: *We've agreed to keep things sexual, right Daisy?*

I clear my throat and nod weakly.

He's sitting across the living room from me, smiling with his perfect mouth and perfect dimple, wearing that awful cobalt blue sweater. It's beautiful. I want to maul him.

"Yup. Yeah. Agreed. Let's get this show on the road."

The next hour is spent in hell. I'm positioned between Patrick and Mrs. Thatcher, and though I love Mrs. Thatcher, I can't get a word in edgewise with her because Patrick is doing his best to monopolize my time. Kelly meanwhile, has sandwiched herself between Lucas and our dusty bookshelf. There was no chair there, but she dragged one over. It's uncomfortable, but she doesn't mind. She stays close to Lucas and I didn't notice it before, but her dress is really low cut. Every time she leans in close to talk to him, her boobs graze his arm. I want to announce an open casting call for the church's Christmas play so she will be compelled to leave.

No one lets up on me or Lucas, and they watch us like hawks. It's as if we're a reboot season of a long-canceled TV show, and they're watching to see if it's still just as good. I spite them by staying on my best behavior. Standing, I take my turn in charades. Patrick is my partner and he's supposed to guess what movie title I'm miming, but his guesses make no sense.

"Um…uhh…*The Godfather*?! No…*Finding Nemo*!"

I look back at Lucas and he mouths, "*Star Wars*."

I drop my imaginary lightsaber and stand frozen. I'm back in that exam room on my knees with the taste of him in my mouth. Lucas knows it. He tilts his head and smiles. The buzzer chimes and we lose another round.

"We'll get them next time, Daisy!" Patrick says, chipper.

"You guys are down by ten points," Madeleine points out, then sees my frown and adds, "But I guess anything's possible."

Kelly and Lucas are in the lead and Dr. McCormick says they make a great team. I'm sick of playing and maybe I grumble a little too loudly as I go back to my seat.

"Don't be a sore loser, Daisy," my mom says in front of everyone.

My cheeks burn.

"Reminds me of the time Lucas beat her out for preschool line leader," Mrs. Thatcher says with a laugh. "She was so furious."

Dr. McCormick and my mom are up next and I eye the stairs, wondering how awkward it would be if I left in the middle of game night. I nearly do it, but then it's Lucas and Kelly's turn again and I watch them because this twisting sensation in my stomach is new. It's new and it hurts. I focus on it as Kelly mimes *Alice in Wonderland* and Lucas guesses it in record time. Kelly squeals and throws herself into his arms. I leap up from my chair like I've been personally violated and everyone whips around to watch me, waiting for me to react.

"Exc…excuse me," I mumble. "Not feeling well."

Maybe I actually am ill because my stomach really does hurt. I go up into my bathroom upstairs and lean over the toilet, waiting to throw up—and then I realize with a jolt that it's not nausea I'm suffering from. It's something worse.

"Daisy?" Lucas knocks on my bedroom door and I flush the empty toilet and then walk out to open it.

"Need a doctor?" He grins.

He's standing on the threshold, holding a box of crackers and a glass of water.

Like that will fix my problem.

"Are you okay?"

"Peachy," I say, stepping back and leaving the door open for him. The invitation is clear: he can come in if he wants. In 28 years, he has never been inside my room. I watch as he steps in and closes the door behind him. He's a giant stepping into a doll house; my things seem small and childish compared to him. He eyes the trophies and ribbons adorning the walls, the pieces missing from his own collection. He smiles as he passes by the row of plaques from our high school science fairs. My shelves are stuffed full of old college textbooks. The poster above my bed doesn't depict a boy band or one of the Twilight characters; it's an anatomical diagram of the human heart.

I sit, watching him inspect my things from my perch on my twin bed, and when he finally turns to me, his gaze falls down my body, onto the small bed.

I panic.

"Madeleine will probably come check on me soon."

His mouth hitches up. He can probably smell my fear.

"Your mom took everyone out back to show off her garden. We've got time."

"How did you sneak away?"

"I volunteered to check on you, considering you're sick."

He sounds amused by the notion.

"I really am."

He moves closer.

"Yeah? What are your symptoms?"

"Tightening in my chest. Faint feeling. Twisting in my stomach. A desire to inflict bodily harm on Kelly."

He hides his smile and drops the water and crackers down on my nightstand. "Just as I feared."

I fall back dramatically across my bed. "I probably won't survive the night, will I?"

The old mattress sinks with his weight as he dips down beside me. For a second, we just sit there on my childhood bed, not touching, respecting house rules, but that doesn't last long.

"Just a few more tests, then we'll know." His hand barely touches my stomach and then he draws a soft circle, twirling the fabric of my dress around his finger. "How about here? Does this hurt?"

I nod and close my eyes. "Yes."

His hand slides up over my ribs and chest until it rests directly over my heart.

"And here?"

I reply with a shaky voice, "Worst it's ever felt."

He leans down and his mouth hits the side of my exposed neck. "*Here?*"

"I'm not sure. Do it one more time."

I feel his smile against my skin as his hand trails down between my legs. He's gathering the silky fabric of my dress in his hands and tugging it up gently. My knees are bared to him. Then my thighs. The bottom of my panties is just barely visible and the cool air hitting that forbidden patch of skin makes me shiver.

Lucas pauses and pulls back, leaving me exposed for

him to peruse.

"Spread your legs," he says.

His words are commanding, but his tone is gentle—so gentle in fact, that I comply. I part my thighs and my dress rides up another few inches, and then it gets worse. Lucas is fingering my panties and sliding them down my thighs. I have to bend my knees so he can tug them down my legs, but my body isn't my own. It listens and does exactly what he wants.

Once I'm naked from the waist down, Lucas pushes off the bed.

I prop myself up on my elbows to watch him move in my room, hungry for his thoughts. What is he thinking as he leans back against my dresser and assesses me cooly? Still clad in his jeans, he's got the advantage. I'm underdressed and yet, I don't make a move to tug down my hemline.

"Show me."

My eyes flick up to him and his attention is between my spread legs. His arms are crossed over his chest. His mouth is a flat line. His eyes are on fire.

"Show me what you used to do in high school. Late at night, when you were all alone. When you should have been sleeping."

I smirk. "Hand me that old calculus textbook and I'll show you."

He barely smiles. "Wrong."

My gaze flickers to the window sheepishly. Could he somehow see in here all those years ago? No. He couldn't. The angle isn't right, and the blinds block silhouettes. Still, he looks so confident, watching me try to recover.

"Is this some fantasy of yours?" I ask.

"A fantasy is a thing imagined. This—you, Daisy Bell,

touching yourself—that's something I want to *see*."

"Your ego truly knows no bounds," I scold. Even so, I don't cover myself.

"Put your hand between your legs."

I arch a brow. My limbs don't move. He doesn't get to be bossy here.

Then he pushes off the dresser and makes a move like he's heading for the door. My arm lifts off the bed and my hand settles against my thigh in record time.

"There," I say, not quite as calmly as I would have hoped.

"The Daisy I knew was never this shy. She never backed down from a challenge."

It's a bald-faced attempt at reverse psychology. He's trying to manipulate me, but it tips his hand. He's growing impatient, desperate.

"Is that what this is?" I sound out of breath. "A challenge?"

"Yes."

My hand slides up my thigh slowly. "But, a challenge for whom?"

When I get close, his jaw tightens. I like it.

"Run a finger up and down."

My gaze flickers to the door. Window. Him. He's leaning forward ever so slightly and I wish he couldn't see how turned on I am. The evidence is sticking to my finger. I do what he tells me because I want to, and because it feels good to touch myself. He's calling the shots, but I'm the one biting my lip. Rolling my hips. Letting my eyes flutter closed.

"Look at me."

I do.

"It's too easy if you close your eyes. You can pretend

you're alone. I want you to know I'm watching."

I realize then that the cobalt blue sweater is deceiving—no Gap model ever told a girl to finger herself. He should be wearing leather. Chains. A mask.

"Daisy?"

"Yes?"

"Dip your finger inside and tell me how it feels."

I blush so hard my skin prickles, but my middle finger is already moving, dragging back and forth across my folds until I gently press inside. Lucas' audible groan spurs me on and I slip my finger in another inch.

I barely hear him reminding me of his order: *tell me how it feels.*

"Tight," I say.

My first word undoes him. He steps away from the dresser and I challenge him by dragging my finger out and back in.

"Warm. Wet."

Three words and Lucas is on me, tugging me until my hips rest on the edge of the bed. He kneels down between my legs and my finger is in his mouth. He licks it clean before releasing it. Then I use that hand to muffle my cries as his head dips down between my thighs. Seeing him there, feeling his breath hit that sensitive skin is sexy on a scale I've never come close to before. His hands hold me open for him, biting into my thighs until I bruise. There's no escaping that first gentle lick. Only a taste, but he wants more.

He kisses the groove at the base of my thigh, the patch of skin just to the left of where I need. He circles the spot and only when my hand is clasped tight over my mouth does he let his tongue run across me. I buck off the bed as he licks higher, swirling his tongue and lapping me up.

Lucas Thatcher has never fucked me, but with his mouth, he comes close.

Lightning ripples through me. I want more, I want it all. His mouth kisses its way across the center of my body. I'm all but spread eagle for him, my hands gripping swaths of blanket on either side of my head. It's the best I can do to root myself down to earth. I feel like I'm falling.

He parts me with one hand and dips back in for more.

"It's too much," I cry, squeezing my eyes closed.

He doesn't agree and he doesn't let up.

"Too—ah! Lucas! It's too much!"

When he adds a finger to the mix, I'm a goner. He pumps it in and out of me, working in time with his mouth. I beg him to continue. I'm promising my first born, the practice, every cent to my name if only he won't stop doing that—right there—with his gloriously long fingers that seem to put out fires I didn't even know were burning.

When I tug my hands through his hair and he hits the spot, I think, *I don't hate Lucas*. I don't hate Lucas at all. His fingers stay inside me as I start to come and my hips are rolling, pushing me up against his mouth.

My orgasm takes on a life of its own. It breaks records and sets new ones. I fight to stay quiet through it, but if I could, I would be shouting Lucas' praises at the top of my lungs.

HEY EVERYONE. TURNS OUT LUCAS REALLY KNOWS WHAT HE'S DOING IN BED.

Maybe it's for the best that I can't. "Wa-water," I croak, pointing to the glass on the bedside table.

Lucas laughs as he grabs it then walks into the bathroom. I hear him splashing water on his face and when he returns, I'm still floating on my post-orgasm high. Nothing is wrong, everything is beautiful...*are those cartoon birds flying around my room?*

I sip the water and hum in appreciation.

Lucas politely tugs my dress down and waits for me to gather my wits. He's dropping a kiss to my cheek when the door swings open and my mom's voice fills the room.

"Daisy! Are you feelOHMYGOD—"

She didn't knock.

WHO DOESN'T KNOCK?

Her shouts are cut short when a ceramic mug shatters on the hardwood. Steaming tea scalds her legs and she winces, but her eyes are locked on us, frozen in the most easily decipherable tableau in history: Lucas hovering over me on my bed, my body flush from an orgasm, my eyes filled with an emotion I'm not quite ready to cop up to.

"DAISY BELL!"

At first, I think she's furious, but then she laughs. And it won't stop. She's stuck in a never-ending loop.

"Mrs. Bell," Lucas says. "Hold on."

He jumps into action and grabs a towel from my bathroom to clean up the spilled tea.

Madeleine and Mrs. Thatcher stand in the doorway behind her like museumgoers. I didn't notice them before.

I leap off my bed and slip on my underwear. I nearly lose my footing, but Lucas catches me at the last second. I'm reclined in his arms like he's dipping me on the dance floor—no doubt, in this pose, we are cute as shit.

"It's not what y'all think," I say.

Lucas tilts me upright and makes sure I have my footing before letting me go. It's a thoughtful gesture and everyone notices.

"Oh, do try to explain your way out of this one," Madeleine says with an evil little smile.

Mrs. Thatcher grins, holds her hands up, and turns for

the stairs. "No need to explain! I didn't see a thing."

"Hey, Patrick! Will you bring a broom up here?" my mom shouts.

"On it!"

I'm mortified. For the next fifteen minutes, the parade continues. My room is a revolving door. Dr. McCormick comes up to make sure my mom's legs aren't badly scalded. Patrick is helping Lucas sweep up ceramic shards and Kelly, bless her heart, comes up and sits obliviously on my bed. In the exact spot where I just lay. My buttcheeks were *right there*.

"Ooh, warm," she chirps, settling in. "Are we playing games up here now?"

I'm tickled by her obliviousness. My mortification turns into resigned amusement, and out of nowhere I start laughing maniacally. Whatever my condition is, it must be infectious, because Madeleine joins in, then my mom, followed by everyone else. Even though I'm embarrassed, I still understand the ridiculousness of it all. It is like walking in and finding Wile E. Coyote and the Roadrunner in bed together.

"Ah-ha-ha, ah-ha, haaa," laughs Kelly. "What are we laughing about again?"

℞
CHAPTER TWENTY-ONE

I was probably wrong to take things this far with Lucas. For much the same reason you don't adopt a baby python because it's cute (*they only grow a few feet, right?*), you don't start fooling around with your lifelong rival just because you're horny. It's all fine and dandy to have a devil-may-care attitude, up until the point that the devil marches into your room, takes off your panties, and shows you just how much he really does care.

Before I started mixing business and pleasure, things were good. I had it all. An even temperament. A mother who could look me in the eyes without giggling. A multi-phase plan to take over Dr. McCormick's practice. I was going places.

Now, I'm down one pair of underwear—I chucked them in the trash after game night—and the only place I'm going is Dairy Queen. Shocker. To my dismay, they aren't open; apparently I'm the only one who needs a tasty treat at 5:45 AM on a Monday.

What is compelling me to stray from a 28-year method with proven results? All I had to do was keep a distance. Become a kickass doctor. Make Lucas cry.

It's Lucas.

He's the one that changed.

The minute he moved back to Hamilton he was all, *look at me with my muscles and my fitted pants*. I once saw him eating quinoa for lunch—QUINOA, a grain he hadn't even known existed the last time I saw him.

I should have realized he was after something, and now, it makes sense. He wasn't kidding when he told me he wanted me to fall in love so that after he's broken my heart, I'll move away and give him the practice. He really thinks that word—that four-letter sissy word—will win him this war.

It's going to take more than one cobalt blue sweater and a handful of accidental orgasms to make me forget who *he* is. What *we* are.

Enemies.

"Game night was fun. We should do it again."

Lucas says that to me when we're both preparing our coffee on Monday morning.

"Which part, exactly?" I ask, radiating my best couldn't-care-less vibe.

He passes me the creamer. "The part where you spread your legs for me."

My mug clatters to the counter as I turn and push him to the side of the small kitchen, out of view of the hallway. "Are you insane? Are you trying to get us fired?"

"We're the only ones in the office."

It's true, we're here ridiculously early. I guess I'm not the only one who couldn't sleep.

"Still, Dr. McCormick probably has this place miked or something."

His gaze drops to my lips. "So stop talking."

Without realizing it, I'm pressed right up against Lucas, hip to hip. My hands are gripping his chest. His hands are wrapped around my waist and I cannot resist.

One kiss won't hurt me.

Two won't either.

Lucas' lips are like a sleeve of Oreos: you know you shouldn't have them at all, but you can't stop with just one taste.

"These kisses aren't for you," I warn him.

"I don't care."

And then he takes over. He picks me up and props me on the kitchen counter. My back hits the cabinets and my butt crushes a few packets of sugar. They sprinkle out onto the floor, but Lucas is tilting my head back and tugging on my bottom lip.

"I can't," I breathe out in between kisses. "Baby python."

"What?" he asks, brushing his lips across my neck.

"Oreos."

The back door opens and the little bells on the knob jingle. Gina is humming a little tune to herself as Lucas and I jump apart and quickly try to restore order to the kitchen. I'm sweeping up the sugar off the ground when she comes around the corner.

"Morning early birds," she says with a tip of her head before continuing on to her desk.

I stand frozen, waiting for her to come back and reprimand us for making out before the sun has fully risen, but she doesn't. For the rest of the morning, I walk around with a shit-eating grin—that is, until my mother shows up and ruins everything.

My mother makes it seem sensible. For the next week, our house will be getting fumigated for termites—or was it roaches? I can't remember. She swore she told me it was a possibility, but I can't for the life of me remember having that conversation with her.

"When I was washing your hair! You don't remember?"

I guess I've been busy lately.

"So there's going to be one of those big circus tents over the house? Where are we going to stay?" I ask.

That's when she pats me on the shoulder and hands over a duffel bag.

"I'm afraid that's a question for *you*, not *we*, sweetie. I have a place for the next week, but you'll have to find somewhere to stay. I'm sure you'll manage!"

I'm 28 and suddenly, an orphan.

"Where are *you* staying?"

She kisses me on the cheek and starts to back away, down the office's hallway. My my, she's in a hurry to leave.

"Oh just with a friend. Call if you need anything. Toodles!"

"You say *toodles* now? Who are you?"

When I make it back to my office, I unzip the duffel back to see what she's packed me. There's a little note up top: *Just the bare essentials! Hope I thought of everything you'll need. Love you, Mom.*

Sure, there are work clothes and my toothbrush, but she also took the liberty of digging through my underwear drawer. Half the bag is filled with lingerie, the kind I buy for myself when it's on sale after Valentine's Day but never actually wear. Where does she think I'll be for the next week? On my honeymoon?

Lucas' voice drifts in from his office next door and the

answer hits me. She thinks I'll be staying with him. What a little meddler. I wouldn't be surprised if that house was completely pest-free and the exterminators were just a ploy. I mean, she didn't even pack my phone charger, but the lace panties? The sheer bra? Those are accounted for.

I zip the bag up, toss it under my desk, and dial Madeleine.

"HAHA. No. Sorry."

That's her reply when I beg her to let me stay with her for a couple days.

"Madeleine! Come ON, you are my best friend. You're supposed to be there for me when I need you."

"Listen, I'd love to have you, but my place isn't really set up for roommates at the moment. There are boxes…I'll probably be bringing guys home most nights…you know the drill. Maybe next week?"

"You realize I'm going to be homeless, right? Like living-under-a-highway-underpass homeless. "

"Where's your sense of adventure?"

"Oh my gosh, are you in on this? YOU ARE, AREN'T YOU?!"

"I don't know what you're talking about. Look, my boss is calling me. I'll talk to you later. Oh, and make sure to send the address for your particular underpass so I can come visit every now and then."

"Hilarious. Bye."

It doesn't take long for word about my situation to spread around the office. My mom told Dr. McCormick who told Mariah and so on. Lucas knows by lunchtime.

"I hear the Lone Star Motel has good rates this time of year," he says, leaning against my doorway.

"Funny you should mention it, I already have a room set up there," I gloat.

"Gross. Daisy, I was kidding. Obviously, you can stay with me, if you want."

I reach for the second half of my turkey sandwich. "No need, Dr. Thatcher. I have it all taken care of. I don't mean to brag, but there's a *garden view* economy suite with my name on it."

Turns out the garden view was a bit of an exaggeration. In my hotel room that evening, I actually have a view of the lumpy parking lot and an *above-ground* pool collapsing in on itself. The pool is filled to the brim with cloudy, blueish green water. Maybe it's a bacterial garden.

I turn from the window and inspect the room. Faded floral comforter. Crumbling popcorn ceilings. Cracked linoleum tile. There's even a handwritten note from the guest who stayed in the room before me: *Watch for crickets at night. They'll getcha.* I can't be sure, but I think there are actual cricket guts smeared on the bottom of the page.

No big deal. It's 6:45 PM. Sure, I can't sit on any of the fabric surfaces in the room for fear of bedbugs, but I can prop myself against the wall until I'm tired enough to fall asleep like that. Ooh, or maybe I'll just go sit on the side of the enameled bathtu—oop, hello there, giant bloodstain pooled around the drain. If you don't mind, I'll just be getting my things now.

Lucas Thatcher, you're about to get yourself a new roommate.

℞

CHAPTER TWENTY-TWO

Lucas doesn't seem surprised to see me standing on his doorstep. He has a water bottle filled with ice in one hand, like he was in the middle of filling it up. He's wearing gym shorts and a t-shirt, and I shiver at the possibilities his waistband hints at.

He steps back and waves me in, like this isn't the most insane idea ever.

"I was about to go to the gym."

"Don't you want to know why I'm here?"

"I know why you're here. That motel is disgusting. I heard they're weeks away from condemning the whole place."

"Sounds about right. Now I know why it's called the lone star—it's the Yelp rating."

His loft is massive, with exposed beams on the ceiling and original shiplap walls. It has an open floor plan so the living room and kitchen are all one big space. The light from the sunset streams in through the industrial-sized windows covering the entire back wall of the loft. It's nice, which throws me for a loop.

I'm still inspecting the place when he takes the duffel bag from my hand and sets it down beside the kitchen island. Then he goes back to filling his water bottle.

I stay right where I am on his welcome mat.

"Hey Lucas, have you heard about that Christmas Eve truce during World War I?"

"When the soldiers on both sides climbed out of their trenches and drunkenly sang Christmas carols and played soccer together?"

I nod. "That's what this is. The minute I move back home, the war continues."

He laughs as he approaches and grabs a small gym bag hanging near the door. "It's not Christmas Eve."

"I'm just saying, don't get too comfortable outside your trench."

"Right. What are you going to do while I'm gone?"

"Probably stand right here, wondering what mistakes have led me to this."

He looks like he's going to lean in and kiss my cheek, but he doesn't. "Well if you ever make it off the welcome mat, make yourself at home."

Ha.

Home.

Home inside Lucas Thatcher's loft—what a ridiculous concept. It's not that I don't want to be there. For years, I dreamed of stepping foot inside a space that belonged to him, but those dreams usually involved a ski mask and a bottle of Nair. He leaves for the gym and I'm there in his space, unsupervised and free to do anything I please. There's a stack of his mail on the kitchen counter. I could root through it and throw away his bills, ruin his credit. On his coffee table sits a worn paperback. I could move his bookmark up a few pages, or write spoilers in the margins. His laptop. His DVR. All of it would be so easy to tamper with, but in the end, I stay right on that welcome mat until he returns from the gym.

The door hits me in the back of the head when he walks in.

"Oh shit. Daisy, sorry."

"Yup. No problem. No, I'm fine. No thanks, not hungry."

He throws the bag of frozen peas back in the freezer when I refuse it.

"I was kidding about you staying on the welcome mat."

"You just left."

"That was 40 minutes ago."

"Yeah, well. I was about to move. I just didn't know where I wanted to go yet."

He walks over and takes me by the shoulders, physically forcing me to step off the mat. I expect the floor to be lava.

"It smells like you," I announce, "but you just moved in. Do you just spray the entire place when you put your cologne on or something?"

"I don't smell anything."

"You wouldn't."

He laughs and turns to face me. "I'm going to make dinner. Do you want to sit at the bar or on the couch?"

He has to ask because if he lets go, I will stay right there in the entryway. Frozen.

"Couch, I guess."

He guides me there and sits me down right in the middle.

"I thought about taking the batteries out of your smoke detectors," I admit, looking up at him as he props a pillow behind my back. He's my caretaker—my caretaker who smells like he just finished working out. I should hate it, but I don't.

He laughs under his breath. "I wouldn't expect anything less."

He starts to straighten, but I grab ahold of his t-shirt and give life to an intrusive thought. "Let's get freaky."

I hold him steady, bent over me and crowding my space.

He smiles. "I was about to make dinner."

"Dinner can wait. I can't."

He doesn't pull away. "Haven't you ever heard that anticipation is the greater part of pleasure?"

"That's stupid."

"I bet you'd be the kid in the experiment that eats the one marshmallow instead of waiting for two."

"Maybe," I say, letting go of his shirt. "But we're adults. We can eat the whole bag if we wanted to."

He leaves me so he can walk back toward the kitchen and start to prepare chicken.

He's making chicken?! Who can eat poultry at a time like this?

"Daisy, you're starting to scare me."

I suppose I do look off, sitting there on the couch with my back straight and my hands flat on my thighs. I've been staring straight ahead, but now I make a conscious effort to lean back and cross my legs. There. I am now a casual houseguest.

"So I know the marshmallows were metaphors for sex, but do you actually have any? For an appetizer?"

"Tell me about your day," he says, ignoring me.

"Good. Fine. I went to work. I'm a doctor, did you know?"

"No." He plays along. "What's that like?"

"I work with this guy. He's hard to like. Everyone in the office thinks so."

"Yeah?"

"He's just the worst."

"How do you manage?"

I turn and we lock eyes over the kitchen island. He's busy sautéing and I'm busy imagining what it would be like if he bent me over that island and pulled up my dress.

"I just sexually assault him and that usually shuts him up."

"Do you want green beans or asparagus?"

"Which cooks faster?"

"Green beans."

"Then that's what I want."

A few minutes later, dinner is ready. It's record timing—so quick, in fact, I'm not surprised that when I cut into my chicken, it's pink in the center.

"Lucas," I say, turning my plate to show him. "It's not cooked all the way through."

He looks up, half in a daze. "I guess I was in a bit of a hurry."

My smile is hidden away as he stands to retrieve my plate along with his. He deposits them both on the kitchen counter, props his hands beside them, and shakes his head. He doesn't move for a good few seconds before I interrupt.

"So dinner was great," I tease.

My eyes light up as he stands and starts to tug off his t-shirt.

"But now I guess it's time for dessert? Yup. I was thinking the same thing."

"Not so fast. I still have to shower."

"Why? Because you just worked out? Because you're still a little hot and sweaty, and you have this masculine musk going on?"

He knows nothing. He is Jon Snow.

"Lucas," I say, releasing a deep breath and circling the kitchen island toward him. "I've asked you politely to have sex with me. Now I only think it's fair that you fulfill that request."

He smirks. "Turn around."

I do as I'm told and warm hands hit my neck. He holds them there, teasing me with a gentle kiss beneath my hair. I think he's about to unzip my dress and get this party going, but then he speaks up.

"Actually, I enjoy making you wait. Let's go to dinner first."

Then his hands slip away.

I laugh, exasperated, and then twist around to face him. "Lucas, come on! All of a sudden you're some kind of gentleman? You want to take me on a date?"

"Sure. Call it whatever you want."

I have half a mind to strip out of my dress and force the issue, but even I have my limits.

"Fine. Luckily for you, I'm a cheap date. Just order a pizza. Meanwhile, *I'm* going to go shower."

Half an hour later, I'm sitting with Lucas on his couch with wet hair, sporting a matching pajama set. It's the most modest thing my mother has packed for me to sleep in and even then, it's not much. The shorts are skimpy and the tank top offers little in the way of boob coverage. Lucas showered too and now he's wearing nothing but flannel pants. The show we have on is boring, some cooking contest on PBS. Neither one of us makes a move to change the channel. I chance a quick glance over and his gaze is on me, burning across my skin. I think my outfit is getting to him, but what does it matter? The moment feels like it's passed, because everything he's done tonight seems to signal one thing: we aren't having sex.

The doorbell rings.

"That's the pizza," I say, hopping up to answer the door.

"I'll get it," Lucas insists, grabbing for his wallet on the kitchen counter.

I choose to ignore him and when we open the door, Micky Childress is standing on Lucas' doorstep holding one large pizza. When he sees me tucked behind Lucas in my glorified lingerie, his eyes go round as the pizza he's toting.

"Daisy Bell?! Lucas Thatcher?!"

Micky is the younger brother of Bobby Childress, a classmate of ours back at Hamilton High. I haven't seen either of them in years, but Micky clearly remembers us.

"Is he holding you prisoner here?" Micky asks, half-kidding as he hands Lucas the pizza. "I can call the police if you need me to."

Lucas shoves a twenty against Micky's chest and pushes him out of the doorway. "Thanks Mick. That'll be all."

"Just blink twice, Daisy! I'll send the SWAT team!"

Lucas shuts the door in his face.

"Nice kid," I say, yanking the pizza box out of Lucas' hands and carrying it over to the island.

"He only wanted to rescue you because you're wearing *that*."

"They're called pajamas."

"That's a pretty liberal way to describe clothes that could fit on my mom's toy poodle."

The box is opened and suddenly, everything is right in the world. The pizza is still warm from the oven. We each extract a piece and don't bother with plates. Instead, we face each other, leaning against the counter, and dig in.

"So anyway, you were saying you're sexually attracted to poodles?"

Lucas shakes his head, concealing his small smile.

"Or was it that you're attracted to me?"

"Eat your pizza."

I laugh and Lucas is fed up. He takes the slice out of my hand and holds it up to my mouth. He's feeding me to shut me up and I'm 100% okay with that. I bite off a big chunk and chew with a confident smirk.

Then I let my gaze fall below his neck, which is a critical mistake in the quest to retain the upper hand. Lucas is shirtless, and whatever exercises he did at the gym must've worked. Really well. He's in great shape with that sort of broad-shouldered, tapered-waist combo that completely kills the female brain. I've never cared about abs until I look down and see the set Lucas has—abs that lead down to flannel pants that have settled low on his hips.

"This counts as dinner, right?"

The look he finally gives me with those dark eyes is the only answer I need.

Holy shit.

In a matter of seconds, there is chaos in his kitchen. Our pizza slices are tossed, forgotten. The box is pushed aside and tips off the island, but we don't care. Lucas picks me up and drops me on the cold granite. It bites the backs of my thighs and I hiss just before his mouth comes down on mine.

My hand wraps around his bare shoulder and tugs him closer, between my spreading thighs. His hands slip up beneath my silky shorts, sliding past my ass and gripping my waist, pulling me closer to the edge of the counter. I'd fall forward if he wasn't holding me up and suddenly we're right back where we were this morning, only now Lucas is yanking my tank top over my head and dropping his mouth to my bare breast. All of it is happening so fast, as if he's choreographed his movements for weeks. I try to play catch-up, slipping my good hand past the waistband of his flannel pants and wrapping around his length.

Beds and candles and stripteases are for people with time and boredom. What we have is *hunger*. We're frantic, and it shows.

I work him with my hand, pumping up and down as he takes one of my nipples between his lips. I cry out and he gently bites. I retaliate by tightening my grip around him.

There's a knock on the door.

"Hey Lucas! I had to go to the car to get your cha—"

Micky Childress is back and Lucas politely tells him to fuck off and keep the change.

"Hey! Thanks!"

I laugh and Lucas takes the opportunity to wrestle my shorts and panties off of me. He tugs and there's a slight rip; I don't know if it's the material or my sanity. For a few seconds, I'm naked on that cold granite, bared entirely for Lucas. He assesses me from top to bottom, taking his time consuming the sight of me. My skin prickles under his appraisal then I reach out for him and he obliges, wrapping me up in his warmth.

He asks if we should move somewhere else—the couch, the bed, the floor?—but it's clear that the island is the perfect height. It comes right up to Lucas' hips and when I spread my legs and let them fall open, he gets his answer. Here. Right now. Pony up, big boy.

I expect him to get naked, to match me in my *au naturale* state, but he only tugs his flannel pants down enough so that my hand is exposed, still wrapped around his length. My eyes widen. I mean, I've seen him before—I tasted him—but from this angle, it feels all too real.

"You realize what we're about to do right?" I ask.

"I have a pretty good guess."

"My chest is tight. I feel woozy."

"I should have had you sign a consent form."

"That's probably a good idea. Can I borrow a pen?"

"Daisy."

"Oh god. This is so strange! Lucas Thatcher is about to have sex with me."

"Yes he is." Lucas laughs, tugging me against his chest. It's an intimate little hug, a reassuring, *I've got you.*

"We can't do this," I say, even as I pull him closer.

"If you want to wait, we—"

"NO! GOD, HAVEN'T YOU BEEN LISTENING AT ALL?!"

At that, I slam my mouth down on his and kiss the ever-loving life out of him. He groans and reciprocates, tugging me forward until my hips are barely resting on the island. We're aligned perfectly, hip to hip, just like I planned. He makes first contact and my heart races as tingles drift up my spine. I want him to get on with it, but he teases me with his touch.

His palm lies flat against my stomach, and goosebumps spread as his thumb brushes down over the heart of my senses. The feather-light swirls might as well be a drumroll, building the intensity until the moment he pulls back and looks between us. I squeeze my eyes closed and curl my toes as he sinks in the first inch. My mouth falls open. Another inch. A tiny squeak escapes me. Another firm thrust and Lucas uses all those hard-earned ab muscles to bury himself inside me to the hilt. I am stretched to oblivion and I tell Lucas.

"Don't move or I'll shatter."

"You'll be fine."

"You'll kill me."

He pulls out gently and I feel him shiver. Of all the symptoms I've ever witnessed, Lucas overcome with pleasure from being inside me is the most compelling.

"Do that again," I plead.

He does, driving back into me and dragging out nice and slow. I wrap my arms around his neck and press my naked chest against his. Hard pectorals complement my feminine curves. Warmth explodes through me, the first sensation that warns of what's to come. He grips my thighs and thrusts faster. If I could talk, my words would come out disjointed from the bouncing, from the power, from the YES RIGHT THERE, LUCAS, YOU GOD.

His hand once again finds its way between my thighs and he adds teasing little circles to the repertoire. The pad of his finger is rough but I like it.

"I'm so close," I tell him, and he continues those sensational circles. He keeps them going at just the right pace, just the right pressure, so every time he glides over that bundle of nerves, pleasure detonates through me. I'm picked up off the counter and shoved up against the pantry door. Lucas uses the angle to leverage himself deeper inside me. He hits a whole new level and I haven't taken a breath in minutes. There's no way to tell if I've died or not, because surely this is exactly what heaven must be like.

For too long, every sensation bombards me and I nearly tap out. It feels like too much. I'm burning up from within and then his thumb swipes once more and I finally flame out. Lucas follows and together, we hold each other up, gasping and quivering and carrying each other to the highest of highs. We don't move from the pantry door. At this point, it's holding me up more than Lucas is. I've got one leg wrapped around his waist and the other just sort of dangling, too weak to hold itself up.

So many words flood the tip of my tongue. Apologies, congratulations. A part of me nearly confesses undying love. For what? I don't know. But then Lucas sets me back on my feet and we lock eyes. It's the first time we've looked at each other in a while and a short burst of laughter spills out of me. I think it's residual pleasure still rippling through me. Lucas smiles too. It's lazy and satisfied.

My stomach hurts while I brush my teeth later. I recognize the feeling: the subtle dread associated with change, mixed with a nice dose of anxiety. It's how I felt this morning before Lucas tricked me into a kitchen make-out session.

I look at myself in the mirror and don't recognize the girl staring back at me. I wipe away the smudges on the glass, and now I do. She is me, sated after having sex with her lifelong rival.

I spit. Continue to brush. Anything to delay the next few minutes from taking place.

I suspect my freak out has something to do with my current living situation as well. In normal circumstances, I would run. I would retreat back to my house and hide beneath my childhood comforter. But I'm stuck. In Lucas' apartment. In his bathroom, using *his* soft hand towel.

He comes in and catches my eyes in the mirror. The feeling in my stomach swells to dangerous territory. I might throw up.

"Where should I put your bag?"

His question is only six words, but there are volumes of

subtext between them.

"Guest room?" I shrug. "Is that where you think it should go?"

"Yeah, that's probably…yeah," he says, hoisting it onto his shoulder.

"Unless you think—"

"No—I mean, you've been through a lot." He nods and walks out. "There's an extra pillow in the hall closet if you need it."

"Thanks," I say, mouth full of toothpaste.

We are two ballerinas tiptoeing around one another.

Even worse, when I slip into the guest room, making less noise than a mouse, I spot the glass of water and book he's left on my nightstand and I sigh. While I was working out a way to shimmy through the bathroom window and escape into the night, Lucas was worried about my hydration and—*dammit*, the book is a psychological thriller, my favorite genre.

Lucas, you manipulative, adorable asshole.

℞
_____

CHAPTER TWENTY-THREE

The next day, Lucas and I are actors, doing our best impressions of *adults cohabitating*. He's flipping pancakes when I walk out of the guest room. I take in the glorious, bare-chested sight of him pouring more batter into the skillet. It's a materialization of a dream every woman has had at least once.

We arrive to work early and divvy up the patients without any arguments. Dr. McCormick is impressed and he says so. Of course, he doesn't know I'm currently shacked up with Lucas, but I don't really see the utility in telling him so.

After work, we leave the practice and stroll across the street to Lucas' apartment while discussing dinner possibilities. I'm hoping for pasta and Lucas was planning on grilled salmon, but he's willing to oblige me. We trot upstairs and he unlocks the door to his loft.

After I've changed out of my work clothes, we uncork a reasonably priced bottle of wine, put the spaghetti on to boil, and take seats on opposite ends of the couch to flip through the month's medical journals. Lucas subscribes to all the best ones and I tell him so.

"You really can't put a price on continuing education,"

he replies.

"Indubitably."

"Besides, the subscriptions are tax-deductible."

Look at us discussing taxes and *not* having wild bouts of hate sex.

"What a savvy businessman you are." I'm not even being sarcastic. "Could you pass the wine?"

Instead of passing me the bottle, he tops off my glass and then his own. The bottle is empty and we are still *adults cohabitating*.

"If you'd like, I could make the pasta sauce," I suggest, standing with my wine.

"Wonderful."

While I pull ingredients out of his refrigerator and pantry, Lucas turns on music. It's cool jazz. Neither of us are actual aficionados, but in this fantasy, we are.

Lucas surprises me by sliding up behind me, offering to help with the sauce. It's not long before he wraps his arms around my middle and spins me around.

"Let's pause on dinner for a second."

"Oh dear, the sauce will burn with talk like that!" I say in an overdone 1950s housewife impression.

He laughs under his breath and tilts my head back to gain access to my neck. He kisses the sensitive little area just beneath my chin.

"I'll make it worth your while," he swears.

I bat at his chest and pretend to put up a fight, but it's clear that our performance art piece is quickly becoming a porno.

I hop up, wrapping my legs around his midsection. He steps toward our previous spot on the kitchen island, and I reprimand him.

"Lucas, for God's sake, the couch this time. I have

bruises from the granite."

I want to lie back and feel his weight on top of me. He carries me there and we tumble down. In seconds, his medical journals are tossed to the ground, crumpled in a heap. His foot collides with his phone and it crashes to the floor. The sound of soft jazz is cut off.

After our fast and dirty pre-dinner romp, we drop the phony act. Instead of swirling wine and discussing international trade deals, we eat soggy pasta with runny sauce while we flip through TV channels, never quite agreeing on what to watch.

"So what do you watch up here when you're all alone?" I ask.

"Mostly the news, or ESPN."

"Wooooow, talk about a shocker. Put it on HGTV—I think *Fixer Upper* is on."

"How many times can you watch Joanna Gaines say '*French doors here*' and '*Put a beam on it*' before it gets old?"

Before I can answer Lucas with *How dare you insult Jo*, my phone rings.

I stand to answer and eye him with disdain.

"H. G. T. V. Just do it."

By the time I reach my room, the call clicks over to voicemail, and I hit play once my door is closed.

"Daisy! It's Damian. How's it going? It's been forever. I'm not surprised to get your voicemail now that you're a big important doctor, but whenever you get the chance, give me a call back. I have an interesting proposition, something I really think you're going to want to hear."

Damian is my oldest friend from college; we met during orientation at Duke. Yes, there *was* a brief romance, but it was far more friendly than amorous. According to Damian, he has that fleeting relationship to thank for discovering he wasn't bi after all, just regular ol' gay. At the time, I didn't know whether to be offended or amused, so I just congratulated him on his self-discovery and we've gone on as friends ever since.

I put on my jacket and head toward the door, too curious to wait until later to call him back.

"I'm going on a walk," I say to Lucas, who is too engrossed in a rerun of *Law and Order: SVU* to offer any more than the real-life equivalent of *kthxbye*.

As I hop down the stairs and tap his name on my phone, I remember that Damian went to work in marketing for a big urgent care conglomerate a few years ago. I wonder if he's enjoying it.

"Damian? It's Daisy." I smile when the call clicks on. "Long time no talk."

"Daisy!" he bellows. "You're going to be happy you called back so quickly."

"Why is that? Are you into girls again?"

"Not even, Daisy. That ship has sailed. It's about something else."

We go through the customary catch-ups and then he jumps right into explaining that since we last spoke, he has worked his way up at a company called MediQuik, a corporation behind some of those shiny clinics that seem to be popping up on every corner these days. Now he's in charge of business development for the entire eastern half of Texas.

"So the point is, I'm overseeing the creation of 75 new locations, one of which will be in Hamilton, Texas. You'd mentioned going back and working there the last time we talked."

"Oh, well I'm flattered that you thought of me," I say

politely, guessing where the conversation is headed. "But I already have a job, Damian."

"I figured, but just hear me out. I want you in charge of the Hamilton clinic."

He pauses for dramatic effect. I'm silent because I'm blindsided.

"It would be *your* practice. We handle appointments, billing, marketing, you name it, all for just a small cut. Patients love it, not to mention doctors—my phone is ringing off the hook with guys looking to get in on this."

"I don't know, it sounds really great, but I never really saw myself in one of those doc-in-the-box type places," I say indifferently. "Again, I'm flattered that you thought of me."

There's a pregnant pause on the other end of the line.

"Well that's the thing—I'm not just calling out of professional courtesy, nor am I trying to flatter you. I'm trying to do you a personal favor."

"What do you mean?"

"Look, I don't want to sound insensitive, but…it's just that mom-and-pop practices tend not to fare too well going up against MediQuiks. I can send you the market data from last year, but the gist is that local offices rarely last more than a year going up against us head to head."

I see. This call isn't so much a business proposition, it's a tsunami warning. The wave is coming; grab a surfboard or be washed away.

"Right, and you're sure my little Hamilton is being considered for this?"

"We're breaking ground next month. Hamilton isn't so little anymore. Our research indicates it's projected to be one of the top prospects for the next fiscal year, and I want you at the helm."

I take a moment to try to consider his offer objectively. On the surface, it gives me everything I originally set out to get.

My own practice.

An opportunity to live and work in Hamilton.

A chance to be rid of Lucas.

In my imagination, I entertain the scenario in which I hand Dr. McCormick my resignation and walk down the road to my new clinic. He would be hurt, but he would have to understand. Lucas would presumably take over the practice, although if what Damian says is true, it wouldn't be for long.

"This is a lot to process. Do you mind if I give you a call back?"

"Of course, take some time. I talked you up to my boss, and he agreed to give you the right of first refusal. We always prefer to recruit bright young doctors from the area rather than moving in a transplant."

Oh god. I realize I'm not the only one in town that fits that description. What if I turn it down and they ask Lucas instead?

"Okay, thanks again Damian."

"No problem. I'll email you the contract—it's only an option, nothing binding. Call me if you have any questions."

As I head back upstairs, my head spins. Damian's proposal came out of left field. My own practice? My own patients? I've been so consumed by the idea of taking over for Dr. McCormick that I never considered the possibility of another practice moving into Hamilton.

I had phases and they were working…well, kind of. For all the nail polish and lattes I've been delivering, the staff doesn't seem to love me any more than Lucas, and Dr.

McCormick definitely doesn't favor me as much as I assumed he would. And, well, Phase III: Force Lucas Out has now sort of morphed into Do Lucas in His Kitchen. Maybe Damian's phone call came at the exact right time. Maybe it's the push I need.

For so long, it was my dream to run my own practice. I thought that's what I would be doing when I first moved back to Hamilton, before Lucas blindsided me. I adjusted my dreams, got used to sharing my workload with him, but maybe now I don't have to. Maybe it's not too late to have everything I always wanted.

"Super secret phone call, eh?" Lucas asks when the door clicks back into its frame.

I glance up and he's right where I left him on the couch, but now there's an open bottle of red wine on the coffee table and two glasses waiting to be filled. I look away.

"Just my mom. She wanted to make sure I had a jacket for the cold front that's supposed to be coming in."

He appraises my answer, as if he somehow knows something is amiss. It would have been more in character for me to tell him to mind his own damn business, and when he nods, I cringe. Lucas believes me, and he shouldn't.

I regret calling Damian back.

R.S. Grey

℞
_____

CHAPTER TWENTY-FOUR

I'm sitting in my office at work. It's 3:15 PM. We don't have another patient for 30 minutes and I've secured the door with a small stool tucked beneath the handle. I feel like a criminal. Maybe I am one.

There's an email sitting at the top of my inbox from Damian. He wasted no time sending over the detailed proposal, complete with an e-signature box at the bottom of a short offer sheet. I glance over the figures, which confirm everything he said on the phone last night.

In towns with similar populations, the average MediQuik clinic doubles its revenue every quarter, while existing practices lose 40-60% of their patient base to attrition. Focus data reports that even the most loyal patients often forgo the familiarity of "hometown" practices in favor of modern perks: same-day visits. No appointment hassles. Keurig machines pouring out hazelnut and French vanilla coffee with the press of a button.

Dr. McCormick hasn't shared more than the basic financials for his practice, but I know enough to guess it wouldn't survive long after a blow like that, especially not with *two* doctors trying to pay the bills and make a living.

I've spent all day going over the offer sheet. I've

already signed it. It's nearly too good to be true. A few weeks ago, I would have sent it back without hesitation. This was always the goal. 11 years of medical training led up to it. Every time I pulled an all-nighter to study, every time I had to skip out on having a social life because I was working double shifts or putting in extra hours in the hospital, every time a patient yelled at me or threw up on me or assumed I was a nurse, I told myself it would all be worth it when I could realize my dream and run my own practice.

Now, I sit frozen, staring at the signed offer, unable to send it back to Damian. At what point did I change? The doctor sitting in my office is not the same woman who was chief resident, top of her class, cutthroat go-getter. Business is business—isn't that what they say? So why am I scared of hurting Lucas?

Of course, I already know the answer, and it's a four-letter sissy word.

There's a knock on my door.

"Dr. Bell?"

Mariah.

I sheepishly shove the stool aside and open the door.

She beams when she sees me. "We were going to do a coffee run. Want anything?"

"Oh, no thanks. I've got enough caffeine in me to wake the dead. Thanks for asking though."

She nods and turns back down the hallway just as Lucas steps out of the kitchen with a glass of water.

"What are you up to?" he asks nonchalantly. From his tone, I can't tell if he's asking a casual *What's up?* or if it's an interrogative, strap-me-to-a-chair-pour-water-on-my-face *What are you up to?* I've tried to play it cool all day, but I know I'm failing.

"Charts," I gulp.

He rolls his eyes and turns, and now I know it wasn't an innocent inquiry. I panic and blurt it out. I am vomiting words.

"Lucas. I got offered another job last night. My own practice."

He turns back slowly, walks over to my office, brows raised with interest. "I knew you were hiding something. Where's the gig?"

"Hamilton."

He seems equal parts surprised and relieved, but it could be the fluorescent lighting playing with his frames.

"With MediQuik," I offer. "They're building a clinic here."

He doesn't need to look over the email figures to know what that means. His slow nod says it all.

For a few seconds, we stand in silence. His gaze falls over my shoulder and I know what he sees. The offer sheet is still up on my computer. Zoomed in. Signed.

"I guess it didn't take very long to think about."

"No. I haven't—"

I know it looks bad. I signed it, but that doesn't mean I've decided to send it. Those are two different things. Right?

"Go ahead." He laughs, sullen. "It's almost too perfect, right? To get rid of me and have your own practice. So take it."

"It's not like that."

"Oh yeah? Is that why I've been getting calls from hospitals all over the country? Apparently I've been sending out my CV. Thanks for that by the way. If you wanted me to leave Hamilton, you should have just asked."

"Lucas—"

221

He's already backing away. He's made up his mind. "It's better this way, Daisy. Really. At least I know where we stand. You're looking out for yourself. Maybe it's time I start doing the same."

"Oh Lucas!" Mariah says, peeping back around the corner. She's likely heard our whole exchange, but she acts innocent enough. "Coffee run. Do you want anything?"

He uses her interruption to escape back down the hallway. I don't hear his reply to her, and the rest of the day he avoids me. I try to corner him between patients, but he's adept at staying busy and out of my way. I think to stand outside his office door until he shows his face, but Dr. McCormick sees me and smiles.

"Not waiting on Lucas are you? He left early, said he had some personal business to attend to."

What personal business? Lucas doesn't have personal business.

When I go back into my office there's a key sitting on my desk with a note: *Use it. I won't be back until later.*

It makes me feel worse because even though Lucas hates me right now, he doesn't want me to be left stranded with no place to go.

I break and call my mom on the way to Lucas' apartment.

She sounds so chipper on the other end of the phone.

"Is there any way we can go back to the house early?" I plead. "Say tonight?"

"Sorry Daisy, not unless you want to huff all those neurotoxins for a few days. Is everything okay? Are you getting on well at Lucas' apartment?"

I'm not surprised she knows about my living arrangements. We're in Hamilton, Texas, after all—word always gets around.

"No, not exactly. I want to go home."

"Not this time, Daisy."

"What?"

"I said not this time. You're too old to be running up to your room to hide from your problems, waiting for them to go away. If something is wrong, you have to work it out with him."

"I have no idea what you're talking about."

"I think you do."

My mom has clearly shacked up with some kind of hippy in the last few days, because she's spouting self-help mumbo jumbo that makes absolutely no sense. I tell her so and she laughs. Then I hang up before she can continue our therapy session.

Even though I have no clue what I will say, I hope to myself that Lucas is home as I unlock the door to his apartment. He wasn't wrong earlier. For 28 years, I've wanted nothing but to annihilate him, and now that I have my chance, I should take it. It's finally checkmate. No one would blame me.

"Lucas?" I call out.

No one answers.

The silence is torture, like a parent who should be yelling but instead sighs and shakes their head in disappointment. I want to tell Lucas he was wrong. That I never, not even for one second contemplated taking that position. That as much as I've hated him, I don't want it to end like this.

I need to say it out loud to believe it myself.

I try his cell phone, a sequence of numbers I have dialed maybe three or four times in my entire life. He doesn't answer. I pace the apartment, looking for clues for where he could have gone. His gym bag isn't hanging by the door and his tennis shoes aren't where he left them yesterday. My guess is that he's working out, but I have no clue where. I could go to every gym in Hamilton? Shout his name from the doorway until they kick me out?

It's a solid plan, but I don't leave. I want to stay right here until he comes home, until he walks through the door and I convince him to hear me out, to try to see that somehow, during all our years of fighting, I've turned into a half-decent human being. I clean out the lint screen in the dryer, I help elderly people cross streets, and I don't stab people in the back, even if I have spent my whole life competing against them in a backstabbing match.

Lucas, where are you?!

I make myself a snack. Change my clothes. Pace. I wander back into his guest bedroom and sit down on the bed, regretting that I chose to sleep in here and not with him the last two nights. It felt like too much, a little desperate. *Oh, sorry. I need a place to stay and a bed to sleep in, how about yours?* It all seems trivial and stupid now. I add it to the list of things I will tell him when he walks through that door.

Which he finally does an hour later.

I'm sitting on the couch, staring at my phone and willing him to call when he walks in. He hangs his gym bag by the door and kicks off his shoes. I stand and wait for him to see me. He pretends I'm invisible and walks into the kitchen to get a glass of water.

"I'm not going to take the job," I volunteer.

I'm hoping my words are a spell. I will say them, Lucas will understand, and bippety-boppety-boo, we will go back to banging on his kitchen counter.

He shakes his head and finally turns so I can see his face. He's defeated. Shoulders slouched. Face crestfallen.

I say the spell again, just in case it didn't work right the first time.

"I *wasn't* going to take the job!"

"You signed the offer, Daisy."

"Lucas, you aren't listening!"

He brushes past me and tries to make it to his room, but I move in front of him and block his path. My hands are pushing against his chest, keeping him in place when he really wants to plow right through me.

"I'm done with the war, Lucas!" I say, wiggling a crude flag I made out of a toothpick and a ripped square of paper towel. "Done. I surrender. Okay? No more!"

He laughs and I know I've said the wrong thing.

"There is no war, Daisy. For me, there never was."

He pushes on my elbows. My arms fold and he passes, just like that.

"What are you talking about?!" I shout after him. "What about the golf, the fruit basket? Oh, and I seem to remember a couple decades of fighting before that too."

"I realized something today, Daisy, something it has taken me 28 years to understand."

"Tell me! C'mon, you can't just walk away from me— from us!"

"There is no *us*, Daisy! You only care about yourself! You think we've been at war for 28 years? Is that what it always was for you? Fighting, for the sake of what? *Fighting*?"

"I…I don't know."

"You've been so blinded by the competition you've built up in your own head, you can't see what's right in front of you—what's been there the whole fucking time!"

"Tell me then, Lucas! I'm here, begging you to talk to me. You can't act as if you didn't fight with me too—you can't pretend you've always wanted this. What about the other girls you dated in college?! What about winter formal girl?"

"Are you kidding me right now?"

The glare he casts my way makes me want to dig my heels in more.

"Why do you think I've never had a serious girlfriend? Huh?" He pushes on. "Why do you think I always broke things off before I came home to Hamilton? It was for YOU! Because I wanted you. Every other relationship I've had has been a futile attempt to get over you. To move on."

His words are sharp little daggers, making me feel worse. I fight against them.

"Oh, come on. You can't just pretend you were Mr. Nice Guy the entire time. Just because you saved the Founder's Day booth and gave me a place to stay, and…never mind. I'm finished. Did you hear that part? The stupid war is over now. No more!"

He doesn't listen. He turns and slams his bedroom door and for a good while, I'm standing on the other side, shouting at the wood. I'm trying to plead with him to talk to me, but when he finally walks back out, overnight bag in hand, I can tell he's not interested in listening. He's more defeated than I've ever seen him.

"You can stay tonight, but then I need you to find your own place."

He's not even talking to me. It's like he's saying, *Apartment, could you please tell Daisy I'm not in the mood to argue and she has to leave.*

"No. Stay. I'll leave. You shouldn't have to leave your own home."

But Lucas is already at the door, tugging it open and shaking his head.

He's gone and my throat hurts from shouting and I realize Lucas never shouted once. When I think back over the years, I'd always assumed our conflict would end with a bang, not silence. Now, we're done, and the quiet is overwhelming. I waved the flag and Lucas left. 28 years have been wiped out in a single evening and worst of all, that exchange couldn't even be classified as a fight. It was a one-sided desperate attempt to get Lucas to see reason.

I stand immobile for too long, because the second I realize I could have fought harder and forced him to stay, his truck isn't parked downstairs anymore. I have no clue where he's gone.

I try his cell phone in vain. Tonight, Lucas is not going to answer my calls.

What now?

My thumbs have been twiddled within an inch of their life and I think I have crazy hair, but I'm too scared to look in the mirror. Instead, I look around my guest room, where Lucas has boxes piled against one of the walls. I asked him about them the other day and he said his mom was cleaning house and told him to come grab his old things if he wanted them or she was putting them in storage. It seemed kind of harsh to me, but now that I see them all piled there, it is quite a lot of stuff to hang on to over the years. I push off the bed and peer down into the first unlabeled box. I keep my hands clasped behind my back, figuring that if I don't touch anything, it's not really an invasion of privacy. Inside the box, there are trophies and ribbons, very much like the ones adorning the wall in my bedroom back home.

The box beside it is full of his old cross country gear, old shoes and worn-in uniforms. There are a few bibs he wore during races, and looking at them, I realize I truly despise cross country. Always did. I only picked up the sport because of Lucas. I smile and move on to the next box. It's a gold mine, filled with home videos. Full of nostalgia, I kneel down close to read the titles, still making sure to not touch anything. Each of the DVDs is carefully labeled, and a few of them say things like *Easter 1989* or *Christmas 1997*. Baby Madeleine is probably the star attraction in all the videos and I have half a mind to watch one of them, but then another stack of videos in the box catches my eye.

Lucas and Daisy Debate Tournament - 2006
L&D Science Fair - 1999
1994 - Lucas and Daisy School Play
Lucas & Daisy Kindergarten Graduation

There are dozens of them, all labeled for me and for Lucas. I decide that if my name is on them, it's not really breaking the privacy rule, right? I snatch the first one in the stack and load it into the DVD player in the living room. The video isn't great, thanks in part to Mrs. Thatcher's apparent videographer policy of *more is more*. She zooms and pans and changes orientations so many times, I'm dizzy by the time I locate the two of us in the frame. It's from one of our last cross country meets our senior year. We've finished racing and Lucas took gold in the men's varsity division. He's holding up his medal for the camera and I'm in the background, talking with Madeleine. Mrs. Thatcher and my mom try to get Lucas and me to pose for a photo, but the look on my face says it all: *Do I have to?* Lucas obviously agrees.

He shakes his head, cheeks red from the race, and lets his medal fall back to his chest. "Mom. *Stop*."

He is eighteen all right, annoyed with our parents and not afraid to show it. He huffs out of the frame and then my mom and Mrs. Thatcher laugh off camera.

"They're so funny."

"I guess you were right—the only people who don't know Lucas loves Daisy are Lucas and Daisy," my mom says, and Mrs. Thatcher agrees.

Wait.

What did she just—

I rewind and watch the clip a half dozen times before I leap off the couch and yank out the DVD.

I hold it in the palm of my hand, studying it before slipping it back into its protective sleep. I listen for sounds of footsteps in the hall, willing Lucas to return, but it's quiet and I'm still alone in his apartment, waiting for him to come home so we can fight. It's what we're best at.

I slip another DVD in and press play. It's labeled *Lucas and Daisy Debate Tournament 2002*, and there *is* a second or two of debate coverage: Lucas and me as precocious middle schoolers, sitting up on the school stage wearing ill-fitting church clothes, but then the video cuts off. Someone recorded over the footage.

"Which red button means record again? Oh! Okay I think it's on. Look into the camera and say your name and how old you are."

It's Mrs. Thatcher's voice, but the shot hasn't settled into place yet. I don't know who she's talking to until she pans to the right and centers on Lucas, sitting on the ground, chopping up pieces of construction paper in their family room.

"Mom, I'm busy."

"Well hi, 'Busy'. I thought your name was Lucas," she replies as only mothers can. "And how old are you?"

He rolls his eyes and stares up into the camera. It nearly punches me in the gut to see this young version of Lucas. Horrible bowl haircut, braces locked in place. His limbs are long and skinny, but even still, he was one of the popular boys in our middle school, a place where awkward phases were to be expected.

"Thirteen."

"And what are you doing down there on the ground?"

"Making something," he says, looking down and getting back to work with his scissors.

Mrs. Thatcher doesn't give up. She keeps the camera aimed on him and prods him for answers.

"Is it a gift?"

"Sorta."

"A gift for whom?"

His spine goes pin straight. "No one."

"You know, it kind of looks like you're cutting out little white flowers."

I can just barely make out the edge of the smile he's hiding from the camera. "Mmhmm."

My heart clenches in my chest and I sit back on my heels, still only a few feet away from the television.

"They look like daisies."

"Mmhmm."

"She's going to love them," Mrs. Thatcher replies.

His gaze flickers up to her. "The dance is next week. I thought I could make her a bouquet to ask her, but some of the guys said not to make it special in case the girl says no."

"And what do you think?"

"I think she would want something special."

In the background, I hear footsteps on the stairs and then Madeleine's voice drifts into the video.

"Hey Mom, can Daisy and I walk to go get some ice cream?"

"Dinner will be ready soon. I'd rather you wait and go

after."

"Whatever. What are you doing Lucas?"

"Don't bother him, Madeleine. Go back upstairs, or play outside."

She doesn't listen. Instead she walks over and crouches down in front of Lucas. Before he can stop her, she holds up one singular daisy made of white and green construction paper. It wilts in her hand. "Are these for—you can't be serious!"

"Madeleine!" Mrs. Thatcher drops the video camera; the room turns sideways and then the video goes black.

I realize then that I remember that day. I recognize the soft blue t-shirt and cargo shorts Lucas is wearing. Madeleine and I played outside, waiting for dinner so we could scarf down our food and then walk to get ice cream.

I remember Madeleine running out of the house with Lucas hot on her heels. She wanted to tell me something, was desperate to get it out, but Lucas spoke first. He told me that since I would probably be going to the dance alone, I'd better go with him so people didn't point and laugh. I walked up and punched him in the eye, right underneath their oak tree, and I got into a hell of a lot of trouble. Even still, I was allowed to go to the dance with Matt Del Rey, and Lucas never showed. All these years, I assumed he'd been grounded for being mean to me. I liked to imagine him at home with cold peas pressed to his bruised face.

The truth…

The truth is much worse.

I notice there is a leak in Lucas' ceiling, and then I realize that it's me. I'm crying, because I am too late. Because Lucas loved me all along and I sent his CV to Hawaii.

I call him again. And again. I dial so many times, I fear

my phone company will think I've gone nuts and cut off my service.

After a while, I realize he must have his phone on *do not disturb* because there's no way anyone in their right mind would ignore this many calls. I try Madeleine and his parents, but they don't know where he is. I'm tempted to check the Lone Star Motel, but it's a long walk from Lucas' apartment and the sun set hours ago.

It becomes clear that I won't reach Lucas tonight.

And then my email pings.

From: lucasthatcher@stanford.edu
To: daisybell@duke.edu
Subject: #352

Over the years, I've written you 351 emails. The first was the week I left for college. I was miserable without you and too much of a coward to ever say it out loud, so I typed it up and saved it to my drafts folder. 11 years later, 351 emails have been added to that folder. Sometimes I treated the emails like a journal, but in reality, I just needed to feel the type of connection with you that one click of the mouse could provide. This is the first one I've ever sent, and it will probably be the last.

Let me tell you what I should have told you then.

For 18 years, I loved you.

Now, I've loved you for 28.

It sounds like quite the accomplishment, but it's always been so easy for me to love you. Through all the pain, all the conflict, I've always known the truth. We cared about each other. Nobody fights over something that doesn't matter—they just walk away. And so, I've always known that if you ever really wanted me to suffer, all you would have to do is just that.

Walk away.

Now I see I was naïve. We were never on the same page. You think I wanted to fight with you because I hate you? Because I want to win? What does it even mean to "win" at this point? What are we fighting for? *The job? Hometown hero?* Over the years I've lost track, and I never really minded because for me, it was never about the war and it was never about beating you. I just wanted to have you any way I could.

I regret letting it go so far. I should have said something ten years ago. I should have never come back to Hamilton. Instead of writing that very first email, I should have walked out of my dorm room and met a girl. Any girl. But it was already too late; not one girl I dated over the years ever challenged me like you did. How could they? My heart, my *fight* was with someone else.

I know you never asked me to sacrifice so much to love you over the years. You proved as much by signing that offer letter. But as you bask in the winner's circle, Daisy, I want you to look back at the doors you've closed behind you and ask yourself one thing.

Was it all worth it?

-Lucas

―

For as long as we've been in conflict, it strikes me that this could be the first real *fight* we've ever had. Lucas' raw hurt and anger leaps out from the computer screen and slices right through me. It's an unrestrained honesty from him that I've never felt before.

I sense flickers of my old self, the desire to lash out at him for waiting so long to tell me this, the urge to call and heap part of the blame for this mess back onto him. *I'm willing to bear the weight of your words, but not the burden of 28 years of silence. That's on you, Lucas.*

But now I can see that my normal inclinations—attack, criticize, insult—they're actually all defense mechanisms, ways to hide feelings from myself that hurt too much to acknowledge. I've reached a point now where it hurts more to leave the truth unspoken.

So instead of continuing a war I'm no longer interested in fighting, I hit *reply* and hope to God it's not too late.

From: daisybell@duke.edu
To: lucasthatcher@stanford.edu
Subject: You're wrong, but for the right reasons.

Please come home so we can talk. You think you have everything figured out, but you're wrong. I wasn't ever going to take that job. Yes, I considered it—would you have respected me if I hadn't? You know it has always been my dream to own my own practice. For years, I worked for that goal, so when it was delivered to me on a silver platter, I had to take a second to think about it.

Would you believe that someone you've known

your whole life is capable of change? I hope so, because I think that's what is happening here. To us. Don't you see? Your email wasn't the 352nd of something, it was the first.

Please let there be a second.

Love,
Daisy

———

My night is spent hitting the refresh button on my browser over and over and over. I hover over my inbox, waiting for a new email to pop up from Lucas, but I'm not shocked that he never replies. The next day, when I go into the office with puffy eyes and droopy shoulders, Dr. McCormick informs me that Lucas has requested the rest of the week off. The anger I'd hoped would dissipate overnight has only grown stronger, and I don't blame him. What seemed like petulant behavior yesterday now seems wholly justified. I had all night to think over my actions and I don't blame Lucas for his anger. I don't blame him for walking out. No wonder he looked defeated. No wonder he didn't put a fight. How tired must he be after 28 years of the same routine? Him putting himself on the line, me completely bulldozing over his feelings. Oblivious. Naïve. Selfish. To think that I might have taken that job is the true lesson in all this. I might have provoked Lucas into action over the years, but he was never really the bad guy.

I was.

I have no clue where Lucas is or how long he intends to ignore me, but I'm not going to give up.

If I want to reach him, I'm going to have to try a little

harder. And I will. Because for 28 years, Lucas tried hard for me.

℞
CHAPTER TWENTY-FIVE

From: daisybell@duke.edu
To: lucasthatcher@stanford.edu
Subject: Hey

Work sucks without you. I had an itch under my cast and now one of your chopsticks is stuck in there. Please call me back, I need a doctor.

———

From: daisybell@duke.edu
To: lucasthatcher@stanford.edu
Subject: Emails

I'm sorry, that was a bad attempt at humor, which is me trying to avoid being honest. Do you still have the other 351 emails? I'd like to read them. Even if you want nothing to do with me, the least you can do is send me those emails. Or are you going to make me write 350 more of these before you respond? It might take a while—I'm having to hit the keyboard with the end of that chopstick to type.

———

From: daisybell@duke.edu
To: lucasthatcher@stanford.edu
Subject: Re: Emails

I'MSORRYI'MSORRYI'MSORRYI'MSORRYI'MSORRYI'M SORRY I'MSORRYI'MSORRY.

PS Are you reading these?

———

From: defnotdaisybell@gmail.com
To: lucasthatcher@stanford.edu
Subject: Hi

Hi, this is uhm, Macy. I'm a sexy single in your area, and I was wondering

Okay, it actually is me. Can we talk? PLEASE? I made this email address in case you blocked my other one. You are so stubborn. Who doesn't reply to emails and phone calls for DAYS?! Are you trying to punish me? I get it, I deserve it, but I want to move past this, and we can't do that if we can't talk.

Also, that chopstick wound is probably infected now, so if we don't talk soon, we'll have to schedule my apology tour around my amputation and recovery.

Daisy

—

From: daisybell@duke.edu
To: lucasthatcher@stanford.edu
Subject: Re: Emails

I'm not giving up.

Daisy

—

I know it will take drastic measures to win Lucas over. Emails and phone calls aren't enough; I'll have to get creative. I dial Madeleine.

"I need your help getting Lucas somewhere on Saturday night."

"Really? It's been too long since you've tormented him. Are you going to pull a prank because—"

"No Madeleine, not this time. Just get him there."

In the old home video, Lucas was planning on asking me to the eighth-grade formal. It'd be way more poetic to pull my little stunt at the same dance, but unfortunately, it's still months away. I don't have months to wait, but luck is on my side when I check and see that there's a sixth-grade Sadie Hawkins dance at the middle school on Saturday night. I volunteer as a chaperone and the organizers reluctantly accept, despite finding it extremely odd considering I don't have a child attending the school. I rattle off a spiel about the school nurse needing backup to treat any dancing injuries now that the kids are bumpin' and grindin' these days.

Finding the dress I wore to the dance all those years ago is not a problem. My mom kept it under plastic over the years because she's a memory hoarder. Sadly, I had a growth spurt in high school and the dress barely covers my belly button. I try zipping up the back, and I swear the zipper cackles when it hits a roadblock a few inches from where it started. I improvise by layering it over a pair of jeans and a long-sleeved t-shirt. I look like an overstuffed sausage sleeve, but Lucas will appreciate the effort. *I hope.*

I find a polaroid from the dance and precisely recreate my hair and makeup, right down to the crunchy curls and smeared red lipstick. I buy Lucas a boutonniere and I wear a matching corsage—which fits nicely over my lime green cast, thank you very much. I purchase a disposable camera and stuff it into my child-sized purse. This is a historical reenactment, people, and I don't skimp on the details.

It all seems like a great idea until I arrive at the dance and parents stare at me in confusion. At first, they probably think I'm the mammoth middle schooler that developed too early, thanks to all the hormones in dairy these days. By the time they realize I'm actually an adult, they look worried that I've taken a quick break from sanity. I smile and move along, never staying in one place too long, lest they grow curious and want to come talk to me or have me committed. Madeleine assures me she is on her way with Lucas, and when my phone buzzes in my hand, I don't even have to glance down to know it's go-time. They're here.

The timing is impeccable. As I make my way to the small stage at the front of the dance floor, I spot the unattended microphone and head straight for it. Across the stage, my eyes lock with those belonging to a pint-sized middle schooler who is beelining for the same destination. She's closer to the mic and scurries to beat me to it. She has flashcards in her hand and a determined expression on her face. She's basically me, 14 years ago.

I turn over my shoulder and see Madeleine all but dragging a disheveled Lucas through the doors. It's clear he doesn't want to be here and has no clue what's going on, but I need him to stay.

"Good evening, ladies and gentlemen!" announces the small girl through the mic.

C'mon, Miss Honor Roll, make it quick.

"Thank you all for coming to the ninth annual Sadie Hawkins dance," she intones, making sure to over-enunciate each and every syllable. "It is time to announce the winners of Mr. and Mrs. Sadie Hawkins Dance 2017!"

She holds for applause that never comes.

Most of the "cool" middle schoolers ignore her, and the half that are listening wear expressions that clearly signal she's seconds from losing them. And I'm seconds from losing Lucas. He's shaking his head and tugging his arm out of Madeleine's grip. He's trying to head back out the door, back to wherever he's been hiding out over the last few days, too stubborn to return any of my phone calls.

"But first, a bit of history," the tiny middle schooler continues. "As you probably know, the Sadie Hawkins dance is an American folk event. It was first featured on a comic strip in the early 1930s and—"

"LUCAS!" I shout through the microphone after wrenching it out of the girl's hand and holding it just above her reach. The mixed reactions from the crowd are silenced by the sharp whine of feedback that issues from the amps.

"Hey! You can't do that!" reprimands the miniature MC. "I'm the student body president *and* chairperson of the dance committee!"

She comes up my elbows, so I'm able to pretend I can't hear her. When she finishes puberty, she'll understand why I have to do what I'm about to do.

"Lucas!" I shout again. He turns and finds me on stage. "Don't leave!"

For a second, he stops fighting and stands there, shocked. Madeleine releases her grip on him and quickly reaches for her cell phone. I hope her phone freezes before she can load Snapchat.

Lucas is in a state I've never seen before. Worn jeans and a t-shirt. Day old stubble and disheveled hair sort of shooting in every direction. He's clearly spent the last few days in hell, probably trying to convince himself to finally get over me. I pray I'm not too late.

"You have to listen to me," I continue. "That thing with the job was a misunderstanding."

My words are weak and he knows it. Sure, he probably wasn't thrilled to learn he might be out of a job, but I know deep down it was never about work. It was about *me*. He's a mess because he thinks he's wasted half his life loving someone that would casually stab him in the back. He shakes his head and starts to back up and I know what I have to do. I shout into the microphone and it rings sharply in everyone's ears.

"I LOVE YOU, LUCAS THATCHER!"

All is quiet. The entire school cafeteria has been momentarily silenced by my desperate outburst. A wolf-whistle breaks the spell and a few kids giggle, but Lucas has paused once again. He's looking back at me, waiting for me to continue.

"I love you, which seems crazy because up until about four days ago, I really thought I hated you. But when you think about it, love and hate aren't so very different, right? To love someone is to strive to be a better person for them, and isn't that what our hateful little competition has been about the whole time?"

"Booooo!!!" a few middle school boys shout. "Get a room, grandma!"

I forge ahead.

"I feel so stupid because it took me so long to see it, but I see it now. You've loved me from the very beginning and I think everyone knew it but me. I couldn't see it because I was so selfish, caught up in my own silly need to win every battle with you, but this whole time, you've been patient. You've played the games with me because that's what I needed, but your heart was never in it. You were never trying to take me down. You were in love with me."

"Get off stage, weirdo!" another boy shouts.

"And I know it took me a really long time to see that, like an embarrassing amount of time, but now I understand and I'm not going to let you walk away from us. That's why I'm dressed like this! I have a boutonniere! A corsage! I want to go back in time and make things right!"

A chaperone has come up onto the stage behind me and is trying to wrest the microphone out of my hand. I'm seconds away from being carted out of the dance in handcuffs.

"Hey! Stop. I just have one more—"

"Ma'am, you have to get off stage."

"Lucas!" I shout right before the mic is ripped out of my hand. "If it's not already clear, you're *my* Mr. Sadie Hawkins 2017!"

"Those are *not* the official results!" squeals the small student body president, still tugging on the microphone cord.

The middle school's resource officer moves very quickly for such an elderly man. Within seconds, he's pulled me off stage and with the help of the chaperone, they've got my hands pulled behind my back, held together by a zip tie.

"Sorry about this, Daisy."

I turn over my shoulder and recognize Tiffany Gaw, an old friend from the neighborhood. I forgot she taught at the middle school. She's the one who helped detain me.

"Oh, hey there Tiffany. How ya been?"

"Not bad. I mean, compared to you, I guess I've been pretty good," she jokes before quickly apologizing. I tell her not to worry about it—she has a point.

"Um, excuse me!" Tiny middle schooler is back, huffing harder than ever. "I'm here to press charges."

The officer shakes his head. "I'm afraid this here is a catch and release situation, missy. Nothin' really illegal about embarrassing yourself in front of children."

"Daisy!" Madeleine shouts melodramatically, running through the crowd to get to me. "Oh my god officer, don't take her to the big house, she'd never last! Will I be your one phone call from jail, Daisy?! Oh hey, Tiffany."

"Hey Madeleine."

"So is she going downtown? To the slammer?" Madeleine asks.

The officer looks up at me. "If I cut this tie, you're not going to run back on stage and continue to ruin the dance are you?"

I look up and see Lucas hovering in the periphery of the group, watching the scene and wearing a smile. It's small, but it's there, and when his eyes lock with mine, there's no evidence of hatred anymore, just amusement. It's the answer I needed.

"No. I swear I'm done."

"Right, well, just to show those kids and their parents that I'm not letting you off easy, I'mma cart you out of here like this and then I'll cut you loose outside."

"Seems fair."

"This is an injustice," mumbles the middle schooler before retrieving the microphone and attempting to regain the crowd's attention.

I'm led out of the dance to a chorus of cheers and boos. The very same boys who taunted me on stage now think I am cooler than cool in my handcuffed state. My street cred has doubled.

In all, taking over the stage at a middle school dance probably won't go down as my most brilliant idea. I'm sure word will spread that I've gone off my rocker and am not suitable to practice medicine. Dr. McCormick will likely want to have a word with me at work on Monday, but I'll explain my reasonings and I have no doubt his eyes will be moist by the end of it—not only because he's a big softie, but because like most everyone in our life, I suspect he has secretly been rooting for Lucas and me all along.

Oh, right. Lucas.

Apparently the love of my life.

I laugh because to me, it is still funny.

I look back just as Lucas catches up with me and the security guard. He's still wearing that secret smile and I want to throw my arms around him and hug him, but I'm handcuffed. A criminal.

"All right, miss," the guard says, "If I catch you within twenty feet of that dance, I'll handcuff you for good. You hear me?"

"Yes sir. I've learned my lesson."

Lucas arches a brow, watching the exchange and probably enjoying it all a little too much. Once my hands have been cut free, I roll them out and rub my wrists like I've been tied up for years, not minutes.

"I thought he was going to take me down to the clink," I

say, chancing a glance at Lucas. I don't want him to bolt now that I'm not in danger of being arrested anymore.

"You're wacko," he says, stepping closer.

But there's adoration in his words and I think there always has been, but now I can hear it. I'm finally listening.

"I've missed you."

He tilts his head. "Yeah?"

"Of course. I ate all the food in your apartment. I need you to come back and buy more."

He laughs and reaches out. With one hand around my neck, he tugs me close and pulls me to his chest. I close my eyes and inhale. "Charming."

"I'm really sorry," I say against his shirt. "That thing with the CVs got out of hand. I never really wanted you to leave."

"I know."

"Where have you been the last few days?" I ask.

"Hiding out at Madeleine's. Looking for jobs."

I pull back so I can look up at him. "What?! Lucas c'mon, don't be silly. Obviously you have to stay at Dr. McCormick's."

"Doesn't look like that's an option. You said it yourself."

"I turned down the job. I want us both to stay at Dr. McCormick's."

"I appreciate the gesture, but…does it even matter?"

"I also have a really brilliant plan for how we can take down MediQuik."

"Yeah?"

"Step one is simple: we work together."

"Has hell frozen over?"

"No, hear me out. We were able to accomplish quite a bit competing against one another all these years. Just think what would happen if we were on the same team."

"What do you have in mind?"

"Oh a ton! I've been thinking it over the last few days. Ways to smash them. Ways to bury them. Ways to—"

"Is any of it legal?"

"Oh, right. Well, I guess we'll have to go back the drawing board."

He nods and steps back, giving himself a little bit of space. It's like he's still in shock at what's transpired and he's not quite ready to jump back in with both feet. After so many years, I've conditioned him to be reserved, and I can't force him to trust me right away—though that's exactly what I want.

We wave goodbye to Madeleine—she wants to stay behind and chat with Tiffany—and then start to walk toward the parking lot. There's space between us, a gulf really, and though I want to reach for his hand, I don't.

He's quiet. Contemplative. I'm scared he's talking himself out of forgiving me, or worse, building up some kind of goodbye speech. So, before he can unwind the thoughts swirling around his stubborn head, I speak first.

"I realized I loved you before you left."

His gaze stays straight ahead, but I watch his mouth tighten into a flat line. He's heard me.

"I don't know if that matters to you, but I thought you should know. It didn't take you leaving or us having a massive blowup for me to realize what I felt for you. I was sitting in my office, staring at that signed offer sheet and wondering why I couldn't send it back to Damian. Owning my own practice has always been my dream and yet, I was frozen in place, stuck right on the precipice of realizing the truth."

He nods, understanding. "And then Mariah knocked on

your door…"

"And then Mariah knocked on my door," I echo. "I won't go into the details of that offer or why I didn't turn it down the first second it was presented to me. I don't think it matters anymore. I just wanted you to know that I loved you before you walked away."

He looks over to me and studies me.

"Of course I'd have realized it much sooner, but I'm really flawed. Chock full of them really. I'm stubborn and can apparently be quite self-centered. I'm going to work on that."

The tip of his mouth turns up. It's hardly a smile at all, but then he shakes his head and reaches out for me. He closes the gap between us and tucks me under his arm so we can walk in tandem to his truck.

He's still so quiet. I really need him to speak.

Namely I want to hear those three little sissy words from Lucas.

Three words that have never felt so important.

"You know, you can say it. I'm kind of waiting for you to say it."

"What?"

He opens the passenger side door so I can hop in, but I don't.

"The declaration thing, about *your* feelings…"

"Oh? You think I still love you?"

My heart sinks.

"Lucas! I just got myself arrested at a middle school! The least you can do is say it."

He smirks and moves closer, pinning me up against the side of the truck. "This was all part of my plan, Daisy. Remember?"

He takes another step toward me and I hold my breath

as his hips brush against mine. He bends low, caging me in with one hand over my head and the other on my neck, brushing aside a few strands of hair. His warm breath hits my exposed skin and a shiver runs down my spine. I tilt my head, giving him consent, but he lingers. Teasing me. I wrap my hand around his bicep, contemplating taking matters into my own hands just before he presses a kiss to my neck, just below my ear. "I came back to Hamilton to woo you, make you fall in love…"

I squeeze my eyes closed and think of Lauryn Hill because he's killing me. Softly. With his words.

"I can't believe you fell for it."

I squeeze his biceps. It's a warning.

He laughs under his breath and pulls away. "Of course I love you, Daisy." He tugs his hand through his hair, looks away, then back. "I mean, come on, I've loved you since I knew what love meant."

"So what about all those times you tormented me?"

He wipes away his smile. "Most of the time people get to leave their hometown and reinvent themselves during college, but you know everything about me, the good, the bag, and the ugly. So yeah, at times, I didn't really know how to show it, but rest assured, it's always been you."

I think an entire hoard of butterflies has been set loose in my stomach.

The car ride to my mom's house is a wild one. I'm rattling off event after event from our childhood, trying to see it through his eyes.

"How about during swim practice?! When I heard you tell Greg Oliver I smelled like a goat?"

He shrugs. "He liked you and I didn't want him to. I was seven."

"Debate practice when you refused to be on my team?"

"You wouldn't have been on mine. We both know it wasn't fun unless we were competing against each other."

Much of our lives follow this pattern, and I'm not surprised to find that he too thought college and medical school would heal him. All those years ago, I assumed moving away would allow me to escape him, and he'd assumed the same. Fortunately, we were both wrong.

"What do you need at your mom's house?" he asks as we pull onto our street.

"The rest of my stuff. They finished fumigating yesterday."

He nods, understanding. "Going to move into my guest bedroom permanently?"

I smirk. "I thought I'd try out your bed for a change."

I don't have to look to know he's grinning as he pulls up in front of my childhood home. There are two cars parked in my mom's driveway: her small sedan and an old black suburban.

We both recognize it right away.

"Is that Dr. McCormick's car?"

I shake my head as I hop out. "It can't be."

I walk up the path and see the TV on through the living room window. I have a house key, but I left it back at Lucas' apartment. I'm about to knock or ring the doorbell when I see Dr. McCormick walk out of the kitchen with two glasses of wine in hand. He heads right over to *my* couch and plops down beside *my* mom. She takes the wine and kisses him as if it's the most natural thing in the world.

What. The. Hell.

"What are you doing?" Lucas asks behind me. "Just knock."

But then they're kissing more and—

"Oh my god." I jump and spin around, fleeing back

down the path. "RUN. RUN!"

"What's wrong! What's going on?"

"Dr. McCormick is in there! Kissing my mom!"

"No shit? Wow, you *were* committed to taking over the practice. I didn't even think of getting my mom to seduce Dr. McCormick."

"I didn't either! Oh my god. I need to get that image out of my head."

I leap back into his truck and slam the door closed behind me. I can't look back for fear that they've caught us snooping.

Lucas is laughing in the driver's seat. "You know it's totally normal, right? Your mom has been single forever, and Dr. McCormick is a good guy."

He's right. Of course he is. My mom deserves to be happy, and in some twisted universe, she and Dr. McCormick do make a very cute couple, but I don't want to think about that at the moment.

"I just saw them French kissing, Lucas—give me a second to wrap my head around it."

"Do you think you'll have to start calling him Dad at work?"

"Oh my god. STOP!"

He starts the truck.

"So I guess we aren't getting your stuff tonight?"

"Absolutely not."

"You're still moving in though, right?"

"Of course! I don't think I can ever sit on that couch again!"

He puts the truck in drive. "Good, then let's go home. I think I have an old shirt you can wear."

R̲x̲

CHAPTER TWENTY-SIX

Lucas and I spend the rest of the weekend locked in his room, barely coming up for air or food. By Monday morning, there's a distinct musk clinging to his bedding and a half dozen empty boxes of Toaster Strudels and Eggo Waffles strewn around the kitchen floor. We are animals.

"You clean up the boxes," Lucas says. "I'll throw the sheets in the wash."

"Okay, and don't forget, we need to get Dr. McCormick a coffee on the way to the office!" I shout from the shower. "In case word got out about my stint in the criminal justice system."

"What if he fires you?"

"Well I already declared war on MediQuik, so I'll probably just stay here in bed, scheming and waiting for you to come home every day."

"You'd get bored."

I turn off the shower and hop out.

"He won't fire me."

Lucas is at the sink, spitting out toothpaste, and when he sees me stepping out of the shower, dripping wet, I swear he starts to salivate. He turns and assesses me just before I wrap the towel around my midsection.

"Don't even think about it." I level him with a hard glare. "We'll be late."

"What's the point of living together if we don't have sex before work?"

He asks this like it's a legitimate question.

"We already had sex this morning, Lucas. And about three hundred times in the last two days."

"We have to make up for lost time." He smirks and my stomach clenches. I know it wouldn't be hard to convince myself that round two is a good idea, so I flee from the bathroom and lock myself in his bedroom so I can start to pull myself together.

He knocks on the door. "Hey, you have to let me in. I need to get dressed too."

"I don't trust you."

"We're mature adults, Daisy. I'm not going to throw you onto the bed and ravish you."

I spare a quick glance at the bare mattress. It's too tempting, so I don't unlock the door until I'm dressed.

"I could still hike up that skirt," Lucas warns as I pass.

I bat his hand away and head to the kitchen to rifle through his cabinets. I wasn't kidding about eating all of his food. We'll have to do a grocery store run after work. Because that's what we do now. We go to the grocery store together like a...couple. Our mothers wouldn't believe it if they saw it.

On the way to work, I psych myself up, trying to think up explanations for the questions Dr. McCormick will have. Whether I agree with it or not, doctors are held to higher standards, and it makes sense. No one wants to be treated by a physician who is mentally unstable—but I'm not. I will plead temporary insanity due to the stress of nearly losing Lucas for good. Dr. McCormick will understand. Also, the fresh coffee from Hamilton Brew should help dull his anger.

I have it all planned.

Dr. McCormick is in his office, waiting for me when we arrive.

"Good morning, Dr. McCormick."

He looks up from his desk, which is even messier than usual. I swear there are more files piled there than up front in reception. He swears he is able to keep it organized in his mind, but I have my doubts.

"Come in, come in. I have something I want to talk to you two about."

The talk. Of course. I knew it was coming. It's why I put an extra packet of sugar in his hazelnut coffee.

"Right. Here—I brought you this."

He takes a quick sip and then motions for us to have a seat. He follows and for a few seconds we're blocked from one another by the mountain of files on his desk.

He shuffles a few things around, and at last, we can see him, looking a little weary, probably disappointed.

"Before you start, you should know I never meant to misrepresent the practice Saturday night," I begin. "I had no choice. My actions, while seemingly childish, were of utmost importance."

He eyes me, confused, then laughs in recognition. "Oh, you're talking about the middle school dance thing?"

I gulp. He's about to give me my walking papers. Report me to the medical board. What will Lucas think? How long will we last if I'm not working, or if I have to move?

"Yes. Like I said, it was a tiny lapse in judgement—"

He interrupts me. "That's not why I called you in here, though frankly, I'm surprised that's all it took for you to win Lucas over. I figured it would take some sort of miracle after what you've put each other through over the years."

I don't argue. I'm a little too stunned for words.

Lucas reaches for my hand to reassure me.

"I called the two of you in here because two weeks from now, I will no longer be working here at McCormick Family Practice."

"You're shutting down?!" I gasp.

I spiral into a panic. He must have heard about MediQuik.

He frowns. "No. I'm retiring."

"But why early? Do you think we can't compete against MediQuik?"

Lucas squeezes my hand. "Daisy, let's just hear the man out."

"As you know, my original plan was to stay on a little longer," Dr. McCormick continues, "to help you two get settled, but I've found the love of my life and I don't want to spend another minute in this office. I have plans. Big plans."

"To be clear, you're talking about my mother, right?"

His eyes widen. "She told you?"

"You're not the only one that can spot love from afar," I reply, sidestepping the make-out session I witnessed altogether. "I'm happy for you guys."

Now, he beams. He is floating on a cloud and I get it. Why would he want to spend another minute cooped up in here? He's been alone nearly half his life and now he's happy. With my mom. Ha, who would have thought?

"We want to buy an RV and travel all over the U.S. Your mom is dying to see Alaska!"

"And the practice?" Lucas asks.

"I'm leaving it to you both."

He says it just like that. No fanfare.

"You can't just give it to us!" I insist.

He rubs his mustache as if only now considering that fact. "Right. Yes. While I don't really find it necessary, if you two insist on a buyout, I'll insist on giving y'all the family discount."

We discuss the nitty gritty details of transitioning the company. I can tell he's been thinking about this for a while, because he already has all the papers in a file from his lawyer.

There will be disgruntled patients, none too pleased to see their beloved doctor retire, but they'll understand when we explain that Dr. McCormick is jetting off into the sunset, behind the wheel of an RV, enjoying a much-deserved vacation…with my hot mom.

He hands off a few packets of paperwork for us to review, but when we walk out of his office a few minutes later, one thing is absolutely clear: Lucas and I have been offered our own practice. We will be co-owners. The thing I'm focused on the most is that prefix: co, meaning joint or joined. That prefix would have sucked the joy out of the moment only a few short weeks ago, but now it makes me smile.

I moved back to Hamilton, Texas, to take over McCormick Family Practice, to beat Lucas as his own game, and to become the better doctor—the better person, once and for all. I assumed that by achieving that goal, I would be cured of my obsession with him. I thought I would finally stop caring about Lucas.

But like so much else, I was wrong about that.

"Does it scare you? To take over the practice with me?" Lucas asks.

He's standing right beside me in the kitchen, waiting for me to step away from the coffee pot so he can pour his own cup.

"It should."

He nods, understanding.

"I mean, the desire to compete with you is like a phantom limb. I'll probably always feel it, even if it's no longer needed. It does kind of feel like an anticlimactic ending to our little war."

"Do you want it to keep going?"

I step back and make room for him, in the kitchen and in my life.

I smile. "No. Do you?"

He shakes his head adamantly. "Of course not."

I nod.

"Do you want to know why?" he asks.

"I'm sure you'll tell me even if I don't."

He looks at me over his shoulder. His dark frames in place. His hair too brown, his smile too tempting. He is a walking dream, and he is mine.

He shrugs. "Yeah. You're right. It goes without saying."

He makes it three steps out into the hallway before I catch up to him, grab his wrist, tug gently.

"Sure, but if you were going to say it…"

He grins and takes his time turning around to face me. I try to bite my lip, to conceal my reaction. It doesn't work.

"Because, Daisy, I won. I have everything I've always wanted."

℞
EPILOGUE

Lucas and I are in a church. He's wearing a tuxedo and I'm wearing a dress that is so poufy, I can hardly stand. We are facing each other on opposite sides of the altar, listening to a preacher drone on and on. I should be paying attention, but I'm watching Lucas. And he's watching me. It's our own private conversation in the middle of the ceremony.

The arch of my brow asks him if he wants to get out of here.

His smirk tells me we have to stay a while.

We're kind of important.

No, not the bride and groom.

We're here for my mom and Dr. McCormick. The two lovebirds are getting hitched. I'm the maid of honor, Lucas is the best man.

For now, I'm happy to be standing off to the side, out of the spotlight. When Lucas and I get married, I want it to be small and intimate, maybe just the two of us.

Our entire lives have been a spectacle. We've made it so. Even now, a year after we took over McCormick Family Practice together and ran MediQuik out of town, we can't go a day without someone referencing our old war. It seems that half the people in town "knew it all along" while the other half still can't believe we love each other. They're placing bets for when it'll all blow up in our faces. Sure, there are still days I want to kill Lucas (the man has a way of getting under my skin), but that passion I feel when we fight is the same passion I feel when Lucas brushes up behind me while I'm cooking dinner, when he wraps his arms around me and makes me forget food even exists.

He is a provocative force and I still haven't come to terms with my love for him. The magnitude of my feelings for my old rival scares me at times. I'll lie in bed, pretending to read and watch him sleep, wondering how many years we'll get like this. I wasted 28 years hating him; it only seems fair that we should get two or three times as long to make it up to ourselves.

He inclines his head, probably wondering what I'm thinking.

It shouldn't be hard to decipher.

With him in that tuxedo, my thoughts have been near the gutter all day.

He smiles and the preacher announces that Dr. McCormick may now kiss the bride. I turn my attention back to the ceremony just in time to see him plop a big ol' smooch on my mom. She swoons, no surprise there—she's nuts, absolutely insane in love with Donny. That's Dr. McCormick's real name, but I refuse to use it. He will always be Dr. McCormick to me—or Dr. Dad, as I've jokingly started calling him.

The crowd cheers. Lucas claps, and then I hold out my mom's bouquet for her so they can descend back down the aisle as a married couple for the first time.

"I love you," she mouths to me just before Dr. McCormick whisks her away.

I couldn't be happier for her. They're a perfect match,

and I have a refrigerator covered in postcards from all their travels to prove it.

Lucas walks to the center of the altar and holds out his elbow for me. I accept it and together, we follow the bride and groom down the aisle.

"How many words of that did you catch?" he whispers.

"Three. Four max."

"Yeah same."

"When we get married let's do it on a beach or something so our guests have something pretty to look at while they're ignoring the vows."

"Yeah," he agrees. "Or we could just do it in a movie theater?"

"Smart. We'll serve popcorn as hors d'oeuvres and play a Bourne movie in the background."

"I like the way you think, Bell."

We reach the back of the church and he kisses my cheek.

"Just so we're clear," I say, "that wasn't a proposal, right?"

He smirks. "No. That's coming later. During the champagne toast."

My eyes go wide. "You wouldn't dare. Not in front of all these people."

He nods. "You're right. Better if I just do it right here. Right now."

He turns to face me.

I'm shaking. He can't be serious. People are exiting the church. Watching us with curiosity. We are practically under a microscope.

But then Lucas cracks a smile.

"What's up?" he asks.

"*Funny.*"

He laughs because he still likes to torture me from time to time. Old habit.

I turn on my heel and head straight for the refreshment table in the corner. He joins me.

"I already have the ring."

I smile. "I know. I found it in your sock drawer when I first moved in and was looking for space for my clothes." I hand him a glass of champagne so we can make way for other guests. "That was a year ago."

He puts his free hand in his pocket. I can't help but wonder if he has the ring on him now.

"Yeah, I've had it for a while."

"How long is 'a while'?"

"I asked my mom for it the same day I found out you were moving back to Hamilton."

He follows up his confession with a long sip of champagne.

"Presumptuous," I say, though my megawatt smile is not so easy to conceal.

"Maybe. I prefer to think of it as *confident*."

We've found ourselves in a small alcove away from the crowds. For the next few minutes it's just he and I. Then, we'll have to continue on to the reception and deliver our toasts. Abuse the bar. Dance the night away.

"You can ask me. I'll say yes."

"I've been waiting for the right time. I want it to be perfect."

"How about tonight when we go home? We'll draw a bath, get out of these stuffy clothes, and you can ask me."

"Isn't it supposed to be a surprise? I don't think you're allowed to dictate the terms of your proposal."

I smile and lean in. He's wearing his signature scent that I love. "While that might work for some people, I think

I've suffered through enough surprises for a lifetime, especially from you."

"Oh really?"

"Yes. How's this one? It turns out my arch nemesis—the man I've despised and competed against since birth—is in fact the love of my life."

"That *is* quite a surprise."

I press a quick kiss to his cheek.

"I was supposed to continue competing against him. I had it penciled in for the next, oh, 40 or 50 years."

"Now what do you have?"

"Hmm, I'm not sure." I wink. "Marriage…children. At least two?"

"Three," he says, wrapping his arms around my waist.

"FOUR," I raise, still making it a contest.

"Easy there, let's start with one and see how it goes."

I smile and take a sip of champagne. "Okay, but where will our bevvy of children live?"

"Maybe a house with a lot more land and a wraparound porch."

"I'd like that."

"And a dog."

"Yes. Definitely a dog."

"Lucas?"

"Yes?"

"I think you should ask me tonight."

"Daisy?"

"Yeah."

"Be quiet so I can ask you now."

And then Lucas Thatcher, the same boy I spent my entire life competing against, drops down to one knee and pulls a little black velvet box out of his front pocket. The same black velvet box I've sneaked a peek at every morning for the last year. I'm surprised it's still intact after all my manhandling.

No one can see us when I start to cry, nodding my head yes over and over again. He slips the vintage diamond on my finger—an heirloom from his mom—and we stay there in that alcove making out like randy teenagers until the MC starts calling our name over the mic. Apparently, we are needed.

I step back, trying in vain to flatten my poufy dress. Dressing me up like a poodle was my mother's idea of a sick joke.

"Do I look okay?" I ask.

"Yes, just a few hairs out of place. Nothing too conspicuous."

I know he's lying. I wipe at my face in vain. "Oh god. My mom will definitely know."

"True, but then again, she's known a lot of things ahead of time."

I laugh, because of course it's true. Just like always. The last two people who knew Lucas and Daisy were going to end up together forever were Lucas and Daisy.

R.S. Grey

ACKNOWLEDGEMENTS

Thank you to Lance for co-writing this project with me. You brought this book to life with your humor and wit, and though it can be a challenge to work and write with your spouse, I like to think we do a pretty good job. I love you.

Thank you to my friends and family for their unwavering love and support. Thank you also to my fellow author friends. Thank you to my readers, especially the Little Reds!

Thank you to my editor, Caitlin, and my proofreader, Jennifer. You're both such a pleasure to work with and I know how fortunate I am to have you both on my team.

Thank you to my agent, Kimberly Brower!

Thank you to all of the bloggers who help spread the word about my books! Vilma's Book Blog, Book Baristas, Angie's Dreamy Reads, Southern Belle Book Blog, Typical Distractions Book Blog, Natasha is a Book Junkie, Rock Stars of Romance, A Bookish Love Affair, Swept Away by Books, Library Cutie, Hopeless Book Lover, and many, many more! You all have been such a cheerleader for me and I am so grateful to each and every one of you!

FIND OTHER BOOKS BY R.S. GREY ON AMAZON

Behind His Lens
With This Heart
Scoring Wilder
The Duet
The Design
The Allure of Julian Lefray
The Allure of Dean Harper
Chasing Spring
The Summer Games: Settling the Score
The Summer Games: Out of Bounds
A Place in the Sun

Made in United States
Cleveland, OH
02 May 2025

16548756R00163